THE DEVIL'S BACKYARD

WARD WEAVER

CONDEMNED ROW

I want to dedicate this book to my Mother, who never, ever stopped having faith in me.

I'd also like to dedicate this story to my Father, who'd always said I'd never amount to much. So, not wanting to disappoint him again,

I just became a human being.

The names of the people in this story, except for my own, have been changed.

*O*n a lonely street far from home, a solemn soldier walks aimlessly, thinking back over his past and, in particular, the last seven years that brought him to this point in his life.

* * *

HAVING BEEN BORN WITH A HEART DEFECT, I HAD TRIED and had been rejected nine times from joining any branch of the Armed Forces. But my determination to prevail drove me on through many obstacles.

That finally came to an end five months ago when I arrived at the California Oakland Induction Center again. I found myself on the fourth floor, sitting before an officer behind a desk with the insignia of a bird on his shoulders.

After introductions and four hours of Commander Meredith, trying to convince me I was on a futile quest, my persistence seemed to win out. Commander Meredith making one last attempt, placed two pieces of paper on his desk and pointing at one said, "Your last chance, son. Pick this paper and no branch of the service will ever bother you..." Switching his pointing to the other paper, he continued, "But choose this one and you're in."

Before he could say another word, I quickly picked up the later paper handing it to him and we sat in silence as he filled it and my medical records out, making me fit for the service.

After writing on one of his business cards, he handed it to me expressing, "I wish we had more like you, son. Keep that card with you and if you ever have trouble with your heart, contact me and I'll have you out of the service within twenty-four hours of hearing from you." I thanked him, shook his hand and left.

I went through basic and advanced training with a few problems, but my desire to succeed drove me on and now I was a fully trained combat engineer with all my worldly possessions in my duffel bag and orders in my pocket, which read: 'Private Ward F. Weaver Jr.; Service number US 56 835 366; report to Ft. Lewis, Washington by May 26th, 1968. Destination: Vietnam.'

The mother of my son and two daughters had divorced me. But my children were heavy on my mind, as was the promise to my parents to make them proud of me.

My training taught me to build roads, airstrips, railroad tracks, and buildings of every kind, then turn around and blow them up. That was the part I loved the most.

I knew my chances of coming back alive were slim, for the Vietnam conflict was just peaking. But this didn't frighten me. If I came back alive, I'd have a career. If not, that was okay too, because life sucked anyways. So, come what may.

The morning wore on and it was getting time to start back to the bus station when suddenly there was the aroma of food cooking in the air. I missed my mother's cooking. So feeling hungry, I headed for a restaurant down the street as people started emerging from homes, probably en route to their jobs.

After eating a hearty meal, I paid and went outside finding myself trying to navigate through more people in one area than I ever experienced before.

While waiting to board my bus, I bought a book just as it was announced, "Bus for all points North now boarding at gate one."

I sat in the back of the bus, placing my bag on the seat beside me. I settled back to read, knowing there were no more layovers before reaching my destination.

I woke to someone shaking my knee, saying, "I think this is where you want to get off soldier. Ft. Lewis, right?"

Opening my eyes, I saw it was the driver. I nodded, rose to my feet, thanked him, and soon was entering the base front gate.

Finding the building I was to report in, I entered and gave my orders to the private sitting behind a desk, then waited.

After reading my papers, he told me, "Go to the adjacent building and find a bed. Keep yourself handy, because you'll be told over the intercom where to go to catch your flight out." I nodded and left.

I entered the next building and with no one around, I took the first bed, laid my bags beside it, and stretched out on its bare mattress. I used the pile of folded blankets, sheets, and pillow to rest my head on, got my book out, and started reading.

I must have fallen asleep, for I awoke to guys entering loudly. I sat up, quickly recognizing one of them. It was Don, my friend from basic and advanced training.

We greeted each other, shaking hands and then sat, sharing stories of what we did during our thirty-day leave.

The next night brought the announcement over the loud-speaker. "Now hear this: If your name is called, get your gear and report to the parade field at the end of the building."

Don and I said, almost simultaneously, "Here we go." And we started laughing, which was cut short as we heard our names called.

Once assembled, we were marched aboard a bus which took us to a waiting Boeing 707.

In the plane, Don and I sat together buckling in and it wasn't long before the engines started. The cabin pressurized and we were moving toward the runway.

As we waited for takeoff, a pretty stewardess informed us over the intercom that we would be flying at forty-two hundred feet at a speed of approximately six hundred miles an hour, which was beyond my comprehension having never flown before.

The takeoff reminded me of a carnival ride until we leveled off. Then it was the smoothest ride I was ever on.

I stopped a stewardess passing and inquired, "Excuse me, but where are the parachutes in case we need them?"

I was very serious and she must have sensed it, asking, "This is your first time flying, huh?" I nodded, looking at her name tag and seeing her name was Sue, as she continued, "Well Mr. Weaver, there are no parachutes. At this speed, if something went wrong, by the time you got one on, we'd be hitting the ground. But relax, we have the best pilots. So enjoy your first plane ride."

As she walked away, I started laughing and Don asked,

"What's so funny?"

I reminisced, "Remember our Airborne Rangers interview?" Don reminded me, "I had K.P. duty that day. But what's that got to do with this?"

I explained, "Just before our individual interview, the Lieutenant gave a group lecture, starting it off with a joke that went like this:

"This guy went through school, top of his class and afterward joined the paratroopers. Taking the test, he always got top grades.

"Being a three-week training course, the first week they jumped off platforms, learning how to land and at the end of the week, he had this down pat.

"For the second week, they were taught to reach up with their right hand, take hold of the ripcord, count to ten, pull, and the parachute opens, bringing them safely to the ground. By the end of the second week, he had this down pat as well.

"For the third week, they were taught that if the chute didn't open, to reach up with their left-hand taking hold of the other cord. Then count to three and pull it to open the Reserve Chute. That would bring you safely to the ground. By the end of the week, he had that down pat, too.

"Now flying at ten thousand feet for their graduation jump, the instructor announced, 'When you land, there will be a truck waiting to bring you back to the base.' So they all jumped.

"The guy took the first cord in his right hand, counted to ten, pulled the cord and waited. But nothing happened. So he quickly took the other cord in his left hand, counted to three and pulled. But still, nothing happened. So looking down at the ground, he said, 'I'll bet that truck won't be there either!'"

Don laughed before inquiring, "What was the interview like?"

"We lined up at the side door of the dayroom and one person would go in, report to the Lieutenant sitting behind a desk, to get his pep talk to join Airborn Rangers. After he left through the front door, the Lieutenant would call the next person in.

Soon it was my turn, so I went in and reported, "Private Weaver Reporting, Sir." I took a break and as the Lieutenant opened his mouth to speak, I interrupted, "Sir, with all due respect, I'm going to save us both a lot of time and energy."

As I took another breath, the Lieutenant interjected,

"What's on your mind, soldier?"

I answered, "Sir, with all due respect, in my opinion only two things fall out of the sky, bird shit and fools! I don't claim to be either."

The Lieutenant replied loudly, "NEXT!" And that was the end of my Airborn Ranger interview.

Don laughed and we passed the time talking or taking turns looking out the window at the moon's reflection glistening off the ocean below.

At one point, Don asked when Sue approached, "What do you think of our stewardess?

I waited until she passed before responding, "I'm going to see if she will give me her address before this flight is over."

Chuckling, Don responded, doubting me, "Right, sure you are."

"Watch me," I replied and fell silent, gathering my courage, which was about to be put to the test as Don elbowed me and I could see Sue returning.

I swallowed hard and stopping her, I asked, to get things started, "Will it be dark for our whole flight?"

Sue told me, "I believe so. Are you enjoying your flight?"

I nodded, inquiring further, "You like being a stewardess?" She nodded, so I asked, building to the big one, "You married?" Sue informed me, "Stewardess' can't be married."

So I swallowed hard and went for it, "Could I get your address and maybe write to each other?"

Expecting to be refused, she surprised me by taking a piece of paper from her pocket. She wrote on it before handing it to me. I thanked her and she nodded, walking away still smiling.

Don gave me a bad time over this until we landed at the Anchorage, Alaska Airport, where we disembarked for a four-hour layover.

Before departing the plane, looking out the window, I could see guys in T-Shirts outdoors. I figured dressed in Class A Uniforms, we wouldn't be cold. But I couldn't have been more wrong. The closer I got to the door, the more intense the cold got. So I put my overcoat on and exited the plane.

I felt almost frozen by the time I got inside the terminal. But once inside, it was comfortable. So we walked around, looking the place over.

I thought about calling my parents, until I found out it would cost six dollars for the first three minutes and three dollars for every minute after.

When the call came to board our flight, we were soon back in the air. I put my seat back, closed my eyes, and drifted off.

I awoke to Don shaking me, saying, "We're landing, buckle up."

"Where are we this time?" I asked wiping the sleep from my eyes.

Don replied, "According to the stewardess, Hong Kong." So I buckled up and soon we were on the ground, exiting the plane.

It was a comfortably warm night and being restricted to the terminal for our hour layover, we moaned a lot, but made the best of it, looking around.

Our total flight, counting layovers, lasted twenty-two hours when the pilot announced over the intercom that we were now approaching Cam Ranh Bay, South Vietnam and he hoped we had enjoyed our flight.

An officer up front stood, picked up the microphone to the intercom and declared, "Listen up men. If the man next to you is asleep, wake him up."

We all looked at each other and soon the officer went on, "Now that I have your attention, I think you all should know that about half of you won't be coming back. So remember your training and you might be one of them that does." Hanging up the microphone, he sat down and we looked at each other again.

It was so quiet the sound of the engines seemed to be magnified. I asked Don, "If I get killed, make sure my body gets home."

Don told me, "Count on it! And the same if I don't make it."

Nodding, we fell silent as I looked out the window with my head full of questions like, 'Would I have a chance to get my rifle and get to a foxhole before being shot?' And 'Why were we still in Class A if we were going to have to fight our way to a foxhole?' Though I had no answers, I was mentally ready for whatever lay ahead.

Sue had been right, we did follow the moon around the world. I spent that time looking hard out the window, trying to see any gunfire on the ground so I'd know how close we were to the fighting. But there wasn't any as I saw the well-lit airstrip.

The closer we got, the more I became convinced the pilot had missed Vietnam altogether. But I figured after landing, it would be cleared up and he would get it right the next time.

To strengthen my belief, when the plane landed, everyone on

the ground was not wearing shirts, nor were they even carrying weapons.

The weather outside was hotter than any climate I had ever been in before. I wondered if it was this hot in the middle of the night, what was it going to be like during the day?

As we were led to a waiting area, several guys greeted us with, "Welcome to Vietnam." So I knew we had truly arrived.

* * *

* * *

Sweat ran down my face and other parts of my body as I looked around, Vietnam was nothing like I had envisioned it. There was sand everywhere. I wondered what other surprising differences about this place there were going to be.

In the waiting area, Don and I found a place where there would be shade during the day. In the Army, waiting could mean any length of time. It was a big part of the Army's way.

We talked to several guys passing and found that we had landed several hours before having even left Ft. Lewis, Washington. I wondered how much time could be gained by following the moon on around the world at the same rate.

The sun rose and the thermometer on the side of the building read eighty degrees. It rose to a hundred and eight by noon.

The next few days were spent eating, sleeping, and doing our best to stay as cool as possible.

On the fourth day, an announcement came over the loudspeaker, "Now hear this! The following men get your gear and report to the airfield . . ." And names started coming, Don and mine among them. So carrying our bags, we followed the others.

A Sergeant with a clipboard stepped before us declaring, "You men are going to Chu Lai as replacements." And we were loaded aboard a C-130 cargo plane where we sat on the floor, back to back of each other as we braced for the takeoff.

Soon we were airborne and the ride wasn't too bad, all things considered. But the best thing was that about thirty minutes later, we were landing.

We departed the plane and were marched about a mile to a row of structures that were about twenty feet wide and maybe some fifty-feet long, with wood four-feet up the sides, then three feet of screen continuing up one more foot of wood and an aluminum roof. There was also a door at each end of the building. The whole thing had a wooden floor, and the complete structure was raised three feet off the sand on stilts. This building was called a Hooch.

We were told to go into the Hooch before us and make ourselves comfortable. That we would be notified of our next assignment and then we were left alone.

We went in, and the place being empty, Don and I took the first couple of cots and placed our bags beside them. Again for the next few days all we did was eat, sleep, and find cool places to spend the day. We were never allowed on the beach, which was just a few hundred meters away. I started wondering when I was going to be allowed in the War I had come over here to fight in? I still hadn't seen anyone carrying a weapon and we had been In Country almost two weeks now.

As I laid on my cot, trying to doze, I looked at my watch and saw it was almost 1900 hours and wondered what was with this 1300 hours, 1700 hours, or 2300 hours. It was called the military way of telling time. I knew 1900 hours was seven o'clock in the evening. So why not just say seven p.m.? And when reporting or recording time, you're supposed to add the word ZULU to the end. It's like the Army learned to tell time from an ancient tribe in deepest Africa. But we were forced to learn it. For in the Army, they claimed there were only three ways of doing anything, the right way, the wrong way, and the Army way. The latter being the only way.

My thoughts were suddenly interrupted by a loud explosion

and I jumped from my bed to someone yelling, "INCOMING!"

I followed the guys outside and a few meters to a Bunker, where we scurried inside

After gathering my thoughts, I inquired, "What in the Hell's going on? Those explosions sound close."

A voice I recognized as Sergeant Hill, who came around once a day to make sure everyone was where they were supposed to be, answered, "The airstrip is under attack."

"ATTACK!" The word rang in my head and here we were without a weapon to defend ourselves. So I asked as another explosion went off, "How long does this generally last?"

He explained, "It depends on if the perimeter is being penetrated or not. As long as this one is lasting, I'd say there's a lot of havoc being raised out there, but …"

I interrupted, "Why don't they give us rifles so we can defend ourselves if needed? As it is, all we can do is throw sand at them if they get this far."

He informed me, "That won't happen. There are three lines of Bunkers for them to go through, so you're safe." But I didn't feel safe. As a matter of fact, I was more worried.

As the explosions continued, I eased out, crawling on top of the Bunker to watch the fireworks. Each explosion was so beautiful, giving off colors of white, green, blue, and yellow with streaks of red and orange. It all reminded me of the Fourth of July. But the fireworks were on the ground rather than in the sky.

A few more explosions and then nothing. So I crawled back into the Bunker, knowing it was over. Don asked, "What did you see out there?"

I explained excitedly, "It was like the Fourth of July. You almost forget about the damage they do. They're so beautiful going off."

Don echoed my previous concern, "When are we getting rifles?"

Remembering what the Sergeant said, I replied arrogantly, "When they are good and ready or we're dead! They don't seem to be in any hurry, that's for sure."

We fell silent as I laid back, closed my eyes, and took a nap.

Don awoke me, saying, "Let's go get some breakfast."

Seeing it was daybreak, I got up and we headed for the mess hall.

Afterward, back in the Hooch, we talked about breaking restrictions and going to the beach. Just let things fall where they may, if we got caught. It would be worth it being in the cool water.

But before we could act upon our decision, an announcement came over the loudspeaker: "Attention, the following men report in front of the row of Hooches to be taken to your new company: Don Cook and Ward Weaver. That's all for this time." So we picked up our bags and headed out.

Sitting on our bags in the back of a pick-up, we took off and after several turns, I had no idea where we were.

Soon we stopped at a gate and on the other side was the first blacktop road I had seen since getting to Vietnam. It was apparent we'd be traveling on it for awhile, which I welcomed.

While we waited for the MP's to pass us, a soldier walked by and I asked, "What highway is that?"

The guy didn't slow down or even look back as he called out, "Highway One." And then he was out of hearing distance.

I had heard it ran North and South the full length of Vietnam and that the Vietcong also planted mines under it.

The gate was opened and we drove through, turning South onto Highway One. We picked up speed, passing Vietnamese walking as well as motorcycles and other small vehicles.

I asked Don, "Don't these people look like kids?"

Before Don could reply, the passenger in the front seat stuck his head through the hole where a window used to be and told us, "Kids that would kill you in a heartbeat, just like their children would and will do if given half a chance."

Except for the mountain range parallel on the West of the highway, the rest of the land was almost flat, except for a six to eight-foot sand dune that appeared now and then to the East of the highway.

After about fifteen minutes of fast traveling, the truck turned abruptly to the right. We stopped at another gate and one M.P. talked to the driver while another came back to check us out. Then we were allowed through the gate.

I noticed we were maybe three hundred meters from the base of a mountain with lots of buildings between us. Shortly we stopped by a guy wearing the insignia of a Specialist Fourth Class who told us to disembark and follow him, which we did.

He led us up an incline and around the end of a long building, which was obviously the motor pool. Behind it, we stopped in front of a Sergeant, who addressed us informally: "Welcome to B Company, 26th Combat Engineers of the American Division, gentlemen. You're both in First Platoon, First squad and you can always find your building by the number on the side of it: 1-1, which will be your home while you're with us. Store your gear inside and report to the supply hut, there . . ." and he pointed at a building on the edge of the knoll we stood on. Then he continued, "Where you'll get your weapon and other gear. Lunch is in half an hour and the mess hall is just below the supply building. You can't miss it." The Sergeant added, turning to leave, "Your building is right behind you." So we headed for it as the Sergeant entered a building marked C.O.

Just inside the Hooch, to the right, was a table with chairs all around it. Down both walls were cots and the only two empty cots were, one, two down to our right, which I took, and the other was three down on our left, which Don headed for.

Lying our bags on them, we were on our way to the supply building.

Entering, there was no one in sight, so we just waited and soon a voice from beyond the shelves called out, "What can I do for you guys?"

Don spoke, "Everything, we just arrived and need whatever it's going to take for us to survive our stay here."

The guy inquired further, still invisible to us, "What's your sizes?"

We told him and then saw his figure darting from between one row of shelves down another, then rush to the counter where he unloaded his arms only to be off again.

The last thing he brought us, were our rifles still wrapped in brown paper, and I knew we had our work cut out for us cleaning the cosmoline from our weapons.

Back in the Hooch, we set to work cleaning and putting everything away. A footlocker under each cot held it all, but our rifle, which we would keep handy at the head of our bed.

We had been issued two blankets, two sheets, a pillow and pillowcase, a mosquito net with poles to construct the net over our cot, four complete changes of jungle fatigues and underwear, two pair of jungle boots, a pistol belt, bayonet and wooden probing knife, and two ammunition pouches with four clips, but I figured on scrounging up several more.

The rest consisted of a bulletproof flak jacket, helmet and its liner, an entrenching tool (shovel), first aid kit, gas mask, and pack straps, along with the rifle cleaning kit.

In the middle of cleaning my rifle, a private came in asking, "Either of you Weaver?" I waved at him and he continued, "Report to the C.O. as soon as possible." Then he was gone.

I finished cleaning my weapon wondering what I had done to get into trouble, for I hadn't even been there a day yet. So when I put my rifle away, I changed clothes and then headed for the C.O.'s Office. Once there, I found myself before the First Sergeant sitting behind a desk looking through a file.

When he didn't look up for a while, I exclaimed, "Private Weaver reporting."

Now the First Sergeant looked up, inquiring, "Is it true you have five years in the lumber industry?"

I replied, "Yes, First Sergeant."

He informed me, "Well then, I'm putting you in charge of our lumber yard. I'll send someone around in a few minutes to show you your new job. You'll have two Vietnamese workers and an interpreter assigned to you. Just turn in your inventory reports once a month, otherwise just give out supplies according to their paperwork. Think you can handle the job?"

"Yes, sir," I replied.

"That's all, you're dismissed," he said, looking back down at the file. So I left.

I didn't know quite how to feel about the change in what I had come over here to do. My mind was racing as I entered the Hooch and Don asked jokingly, "In trouble already?" And he chuckled. I explained what happened, and he declared, "You lucky stiff. Get me on as your assistant."

I did feel lucky and if I could, Don would have his wish. But we both knew it probably wasn't possible, so I didn't reply. I just laid down on my cot and went into deep thought as I waited for my escort.

Strange voices coming in brought me up to a sitting position. I assumed these guys lived here and we were all introducing ourselves, shaking hands, when another guy stuck his head in the door, calling out, "Is one of you Weaver, who's taking over the lumber yard?"

I answered, "Here!" And headed for the door.

As I exited, the guy told me, "I'm to show you around your new job. You ready?" I nodded, following him down the hill and across the sandy dirt road the truck had stopped on, bringing us here.

He stopped us in front of what looked like an outhouse. Upon further observation, I could see it had been an outhouse, now converted into an office. He spoke, pointing at the structure before us, "This is your office." He changed his point to beyond the office, "That's the yard. Do you need to know anything else?"

I felt he didn't want to be there, so shaking my head, said, "I can handle it from here."

He added, "If you need more, I'm Bobby in Building Two." I nodded and he left.

I stood surveying the place, seeing that most of the piles of lumber were toppled over. I was tired and hungry. So looking at my watch, I saw it was already 1400 hours. Lunch had to be over, so I would have to wait until supper. I went back to the Hooch, laid down, and tried to take a nap in the heat.

It must have worked, for I awoke to the Hooch being empty. So I headed for the mess-hall, seeing it was almost 1700 hours. I got in line and soon had my food, looking for a place to sit.

I found Don sitting with several others and he had saved me a seat. I sat and ate, listening to their conversations.

After dark, the heat was always tolerable, making sleep easier as one still would sweat, but less.

The next morning there was a lot of movement and as I dressed, Don asked me cheerfully, "Ready for some breakfast?"

Acknowledging I was, we headed for the mess-hall. At this hour of the morning, the temperature was the most comfortable. Back in the Hooch, I picked up my M-16 and helmet, heading for the supply hut to get what I needed for work.

This time the guy who had gotten our gear when we arrived stood behind the counter reading a magazine. When he looked up from it, I glanced at the name tag on his fatigues, which read Walker, so I said, "Morning Walker. I need some ledgers, pens, and tablets for the lumber yard."

As Walker went to fill my order, he replied, "Call me, Gary."

I interjected, "Mine's Ward." When he brought my stuff, we shook hands and I thanked him before heading for my office.

It was still early, but that was okay, I wanted to look the place over before the workers arrived.

I opened the office door and stepped inside. I doubted the place had ever been cleaned. I saw several inches of dust covering a couple two by twelve's nailed to the back wall to work as a desk. A chair was the other thing in the place. I left my rifle, helmet, and supplies outside. I wanted to clean the place up first.

Some twenty minutes later, I brought everything in. Then I dated a ledger before taking a tablet out to mark down what was available in the yard.

I found there were two yards. The one behind the office was the largest. It contained six oblong metal containers lined up behind the office. They were called Conexes, in which the Army used to ship sandbags and other water perishables by sea.

Each Conex was six feet high, six feet wide and ten feet deep, with metal doors at one end. In three of them I found shelves had been built against the sides and back for maximum storage space. But they were all empty.

The fourth contained assorted sized fifty-pound boxes of nails. The fifth was empty and the sixth had a couple of broken bundles of sandbags.

The rest of the yard was in worse shape than I previously thought, with lumber of every size and length scattered about. In one corner, bundles of sandbags lay scattered around.

The other yard was up a four-foot incline and much smaller, containing a few pieces of PCP landing mat, a small number of different lengths of galvanized pipe, one small roll of cable, and a few various sizes of culvert.

I got back to the office just as the workers arrived. They looked more like teenagers, not even five-foot tall yet, not even weighing a hundred pounds if they were soaking wet, clothes and all.

One of the Vietnamese spoke pretty good English, "I am your interpreter and these are your workers. They don't speak English. My name is Joe, what's yours?"

I told him, "Ward, glad to meet you. I have lots of work to get done, so we might as well get started." Joe just nodded, so I led the way and we cleaned out all the Conexes.

Then we placed the nails in the first one, according to size before putting the sandbags in the last one, neatly. Then we moved to the lumber.

I told Joe, "Now we have to stack the lumber according to size." I could have just stood by while they worked, but that was not in my make-up. Besides, working together, we could then spend the hottest part of the day, doing nothing in the shade.

After lunch, not having found Don, I asked around and was told the squad had gone out on a truck several hours earlier. So I went back to the yard and we worked at a slower pace.

By quitting time, we were finished with the lower yard and I knew the next day we would do the same to the upper one in just a few hours.

After the workers left, I walked around the yard, satisfied with our progress. I was going to make the best, well-stocked yard, catering to every need that came in.

Back in the office, I made a list of the things I thought would be needed for the yard and put the piece of paper in my pocket. I picked up my gear and headed for the Hooch.

Don and three others sat at the table, playing cards when I came in, I asked in general, "How was everyone's day?"

Don spoke first, "We went on a mine sweep. How was your first day on the new job?"

I smiled exclaiming, "Real good, so far. We should have it in good working order by tomorrow and then I'll start stocking it."

Don announced, "If we don't go out tomorrow, I'll come down and check it out." I liked that idea as we went to supper. Cole and Mike joined us and I enjoyed listening about their adventure earlier in the day.

We were served steak this time and mine was the toughest piece of meat I had ever experienced. I inquired, "What kind of meat is this?"

Mike answered, "Water Buffalo. What else?" He stopped eating and after looking around told me, "That's what we call it. There's no one willing to ask the cook to find out for sure. But they'll cook things however you want it, which makes a big difference."

"I'll remember that," I replied and we finished eating.

Back in the Hooch, Mike asked, "Who's going to the movie?"

Surprised, I asked, "You mean they have a theater here?"

Jack spoke now, "Yeah, man, we have everything here. Just grab a chair and your rifle, flak jacket, and we're off. It's a Western tonight, so let's go before the cartoon starts."

We got there before it did and I was surprised at the setup. There was a screen about thirty-five feet wide and maybe twenty-five feet high, perched on poles with a little building about a hundred or so feet away containing the projector. It was all like a miniature drive-in, except that instead of driving your car in, you brought your own chair. Or maybe a theater without walls would be a better description.

We picked a place and just sat down when the cartoon started and for a while, one could forget where he was.

When it was over, everyone picked up their things heading back and en route, Sam asked, "Anyone want to go to the club?"

Several voices blended together with, "You bet!"

I didn't really feel like drinking, so as Don indicated that he was, I told them, "I'm tired. I'm going to bed. Maybe next time. But you all have fun."

The five of them dropped their chairs off in the Hooch and left. I went to bed and soon I was sound asleep.

I awoke to an alarm clock going off. Looking around, I made out John going from bed to bed, waking everyone. As he passed mine, my eyes cleared, I asked, "You do this every morning?"

He informed me, "If I didn't, these guys would sleep until noon." And he moved on to the next bed. I got up, dressed, and soon we were all off to breakfast.

On my way to the office, I stopped a jeep heading in the direction of headquarters. I asked him if he was going there, would he drop off a paper for me. He agreed to, so I gave him the list for the lumber yard and he drove on.

As I figured, long before lunch, we had both yards looking good, so we had the rest of the day free.

I had forgotten about Don coming down to the yard, until I

found him in line at the mess-hall. I asked, "Where were you this morning?"

He smiled, answering, "I just woke up. Sorry, buddy."

I exclaimed, "That's okay, I was pretty busy. How about coming down after lunch and taking a look?"

Don agreed to and there was small talk the rest of the meal.

The one thing we agreed upon was that Vietnam was nothing, so far, like we had imagined it would be.

After lunch, we went directly to the yard, where after the tour of both yards, Don was very impressed. I couldn't pronounce the workers' names, so I had nicknamed them Curly and Moe. I introduced them to Don as Curly, Moe, and Joe. Don laughed at that as he headed for the Hooch.

While sitting with the workers in the shade, a slight breeze came up, making us almost feel wonderful. But we hadn't enjoyed it long before a loaded truck pulled in.

I went to find out what they wanted, but before I could ask, a private handed me a clipboard saying, "Sign this. Where do you want this unloaded?" I signed the paper and led them to where I wanted it. Soon the five of us had the truck empty and on its way.

As the truck left, I noticed another truck waiting for the workers. So I sent them on their way, before going to the office to enter the load into my ledger, then picked up my gear and headed for the Hooch.

Mike and Sam said they were going to the shower. I knew the little four foot by four foot structure just outside our Hooch, with a barrel on top of it, which you filled with many trips up the ladder with pails of water, worked good as a shower. But it wouldn't hold them both, so there had to be another shower they were talking about. I asked about this and was told to get my stuff and they would show me the main shower, so I did and joined them.

It was located just South of the movie area, a long building with two rows of shower heads. It sure beat carrying water up a ladder for showering at the Hooch!

It was nearly 2100 hours when I went to bed and had just dozed off when the world seemed to erupt, shaking me almost out of bed. The explosion was followed by someone yelling, "INCOMING!"

I jumped from my bed in a haze and it took a few seconds for my eyes to clear as several more explosions occurred close by. I grabbed my gear, followed the crowd out the door and across the ground as multiple explosions lit up the night in many areas. Some so close, the ground shook under us.

The Bunker we ended up in was about fifty feet from our front door between Hooches, but it still seemed like a mile away.

I heard someone say, as I made my way into the Bunker, "Damn! They're sure pouring it to us tonight. More so than usual."

I inquired, "You think we'll be attacked by ground troops?"

I heard Mike, who was next to me, answer, "We shouldn't. They just like waking us as a reminder they're out there. Besides, the perimeter Bunkers should take care of any that try to break through. Course, if a number of them do, then we could have our hands full. Night fighting is their specialty, but it's never happened before."

One of the next explosions sounded and felt like it was just outside our Bunker. I didn't know if it was fear or excitement, but I wanted out of the Bunker to watch the rockets go off.

As I heard more explosions, I moved toward the door, which made Don ask, "Where are you going Ward?"

I explained, wondering how he knew it was me, "Out to watch the rockets go off."

Mike spoke up, "They're raining down out there, man. More than ever before and closer than usual. You should wait, just in case we take a direct hit. You'll stand a better chance in here. "But I stuck my head out the door any way and saw the next explosion go off close to a two-man spotter chopper on the pad close by.

Don laid a hand on my shoulder, asking, "What do you see?"

I announced excitedly, "Man, they're beautiful going off." I couldn't think of more to say, I was so spellbound by the fireworks until a period of time passed and there was none.

I heard Mike declare, as a siren went off, "You're crazy, Weaver. You're where you should be, in the lumber yard."

He no sooner fell silent when another voice spoke up, "Okay, it's over. Let's go back to bed." And we all left the Bunker, going off in different directions.

Still excited, I asked Don as we walked, "Did you hear those suckers coming in? They sounded like low whistles, like they were letting you know they were coming and to get out of the way. Yet, at the same time, enticing you to stay where you are.
"

Don just remarked, "You are sick, just like Mike said." And we laughed, walking on. This wasn't the first time I had been called that while watching things blow up.

I thought back to what brought about my love to hearing and seeing things explode. It had started back when I was in the seventh grade, making home-made weapons and explosives.

Two Hooches had been hit, others had sidewall damages due to explosions very close to them.

The next day, in the lumber yard, as we sat in the shade, a truck came in. I met the Sergeant that got out at the door of my office, greeting him with, "Hi, can I help you?"

He replied, handing me some papers, "I'm Sergeant Blackwell. I have a work order for some sandbags. "

It was for only four bundles, so I told him, "Have your driver follow us so we don't have to carry them." He motioned for the truck to follow.

As the workers loaded the truck, Sergeant Blackwell asked me, "You been here long?"

I answered, "This is my third day on the job. I've only been in Country a little over two weeks now."

He replied, "Thought so, I haven't seen you before. What's your name? "

Realizing I hadn't sewn on my name tag, nor rank yet, I told him, "Ward Weaver."

We shook hands as he told me, "Glad to meet you and thanks for the bags." I told him he was welcome.

After signing his paperwork, he left and I went to my office making the entry in my ledger.

I could see, for the most part, this job was going to be boring. I would have to create work to keep busy. But these thoughts no sooner passed when another truck pulled in loaded with sandbags.

A private got out asking where I wanted it unloaded and I told him to follow me and I led him to the far corner of the yard.

As the workers unloaded the truck, I looked at the paperwork. I was to get two hundred and fifty bundles of sandbags.

The guy wasn't talkative, so we just watched the unloading.

After the truck left, we got to work stacking sandbags, finding there were sixty-three bundles more than what had been designated on the work order. We transferred the extra ones to the Conex with the other extras.

The rest of the day was slow. A few people stopped in, asking for material for which they didn't have paperwork for. My being new on the job, I refused them.

The Fourth of July arrived and the only thing that made it any different from any other night came at midnight. All the Bunkers lit up the sky with hand flares of different colors and for about ten minutes, the sky was beautiful. Two weeks later, the captain announced over the speaker that the company was going to the beach. That anyone wanting to go, the trucks would be leaving tomorrow after breakfast.

I was ready to experience the ocean, wondering if it would be warmer than back home due to the hotter weather?

The next morning, one dump truck was loaded with a couple drums which were filled with ice, sodas, and beer before we loaded up and were off to the beach.

The trucks parked near the water. I could see there were very small waves and people were out, possibly a hundred meters. It showed that they were standing on the bottom with their heads still well out of the water.

A fire was built with a metal screen placed over it to cook hot dogs and hamburgers on.

Everyone had brought their air-mattresses and now had them

inflated. We waded out into the surf and found the water much warmer than that at home.

About sixty meters out, I found myself only waist deep. So releasing my mattress, I submerged myself, coming up quickly after having gotten water in my mouth. I found it saltier than back home, as well and thought out loud, as a guy passed me, "I wonder what ocean this is for it to be so much saltier than back home?"

The guy exclaimed, breaking my train of thought, "It's the South China Sea and about the saltiest ocean there is."

When I got out where the others were, I watched as they laid on their mattresses taking hold of the corners and by pulling up, they could catch even the smallest wave and ride them for a very long distance.

It took me a few tries, but soon I got the hang of it. I started to have lots of fun.

After several hours, I towed my mattress to shore and laid on it to keep the sand off me while I was sun-dried.

It didn't take long with the aroma of food cooking to realize how hungry I was. I got up and knew instantly that I had gotten too much sun and would suffer for it later. But right now, I was going to enjoy myself to the max.

I filled my plate with food, got a soda, and went back to my mattress, where I chowed down and it tasted great.

As I laid there resting, letting my food digest, I heard excitement in the distance. I sat up looking around, saw three guys out in the surf with sticks playing with what appeared to be a long rope. So I got a stick and went out to join them.

When I arrived, it wasn't a rope they were playing with. It was a rather long black snake. It was being tossed back and forth with the sticks.

My father had been a snake charmer in a circus before I was born. He had told me that most snakes can't bite under water. This one was spending more time under the water and in the air than on top of the water. The guys made room for me and I joined in as the snake was flipped to me. I quickly returned it in the same manner.

After a while, we heard someone yelling from the beach like a madman. Looking, we saw the Sergeant waving frantically at us to come in. One of the guys commented, "Must be pretty important to have the Sarge that worked up." So we headed in.

One of the guys asked upon arriving, "What's wrong, Sarge?" He looked a little calmer now as he inquired, "Do you guys know what kind of snake that was you were playing with out there?"

The others didn't seem to know and not really knowing myself I exclaimed, "A black snake of some kind."

The Sergeant informed us, "Your right about that part. That's one of the most poisonous snakes over here. It can bite you underwater and you'll be dead before it finishes biting you. You're all lucky this time, but the next . . . " He fell silent for a moment and then began again, "Just more proof that God protects fools. Go and be aware of what you play with from now on. But leave the snakes alone!"

I'd had enough excitement for one day. Going back to my mattress, I stayed in the shade, relaxing and wondering where Don had gone. I knew, however, we would exchange stories on the way back.

Soon a whistle blew and the Sergeant called everyone out of

the water. It was time to head back to the company. We'd had a full day, so air mattresses were deflated and everything was placed on the truck. The area was cleaned up before we loaded up and headed out.

Don and I settled down together, spending the whole trip back comparing notes of our day.

Once in the compound, everything was unloaded and put away before we went to the shower.

Afterward, back in the Hooch, I looked at my watch and saw it was 1620 hours. It was too early for the show, yet too late for anything else. So I just relaxed.

An hour and a half later, I, Don, and several others set out for the movie.

The next morning, when I got to the lumber yard now, suffering with a sunburn from the previous day, I found a truck waiting, loaded with lumber.

The driver's name was Hank and while we waited for the workers, I learned more about Vietnam. Hank was on his second tour here. I couldn't understand his fascination with being here until he explained about the money he was paid plus being raised one rank. That higher rank, he added chuckling, had been lost after hitting a Lieutenant and hospitalizing the officer. We both laughed over that.

Soon the workers showed up, but because I was miserable, I let them unload the truck.

We had several loaded trucks come in during the day and now, both yards were filling nicely.

At quitting time, after the workers were gone, I sat in my office putting the last entry in the ledger when a Sergeant walked in. I inquired, "Can I help you?"

He answered, "Not today. My name's Holt, what's yours?" Though I knew he could see my name tag, I responded anyway,

"Ward Weaver."

We talked about how long I had been in Country. When he mentioned home, I found out he was from Missouri, not far from where my father grew up.

I knew he was leading up to something, but I had time and besides, it was pleasant talking to him. It wasn't long before he got around to what he wanted, "By the way, do you deal in the black market?"

His question didn't alarm me for I had a feeling he wasn't trying to trap me. I could tell he was very interested in the answer to the question, so I replied, "I thought about it, but prefer not to."

Sergeant Holt then responded, "If someone was to need some sandbags and couldn't get the paperwork, would you have extra for them, or do you go strictly by the book?"

I answered without hesitation, "I don't believe in just going by the book, too many rules to keep up with. So I do things according to my feelings, but I always keep my ledger and inventory correct." He seemed puzzled, so I explained further, "I do have extra sandbags. When a load comes in short, I add to it from my stash. But when one is over, I add the extra to what I have put away, understand now?" Sergeant Holt nodded, smiling as I went on, "But as for selling them, I wouldn't feel right about doing that. So my policy's going to be that if you guys are going out to a hot area and need sand-bags, paperwork or not, you're getting them."

I stopped and waited for his reaction, which wasn't long in coming, "My men and I are going out to set up an ambush and it sure would be nice if we had a little more than the natural surroundings for cover. So if you could see clear to help, it would be greatly appreciated. I can't get the paperwork for this kind of operation."

As he stopped, I spoke right up, "When would you like to pick them up?"

He answered surprised, "Whenever it's convenient for you. We're going out tomorrow night."

I told him, "Then I suggest you go get a couple of men. I'll stay here until you get back. That okay with you? "

It was about twenty-five minutes and the Sergeant was back with three men, whom I met outside. After saying hello, I led them to the far Conex where I opened the doors saying, "Get a couple bundles each."

Sergeant Holt quickly interjected, "Just one each." And looking at me added, "We don't need more than this. I appreciate these and don't want to take advantage of your generosity."

I was thankful for this because it showed me he wasn't trying to con me. So I told him, "Whenever you need more, they'll always be available to you and your men."

Sergeant Holt inquired, "You sure I can't get you some . . ."

I interrupted, "Just bring your men back alive and that'll be payment enough, okay?" We shook hands as he agreed to do his best and they were off.

The rest of the week went slow, but smoothly and I didn't see Sergeant Holt as I'd hoped.

That Sunday after breakfast, Don suggested, "Why don't we go into the village and see what's going on?"

34

I was intrigued by the idea of seeing what a Vietnamese village looked like, so we gathered our gear and was off.

A couple hundred meters down Highway One, we caught a ride to the edge of the village. The driver advised we lock and load (meaning to put a bullet in the chamber of our rifle) before entering the village and why, so we thanked him. We pulled the bolt of our weapons back and releasing them, injected a round in the chamber. Then we put the safety on and entered the village.

I bought dolls for my daughters back home, hoping they'd like them. I got a matching silk jacket for my son and me, which had a picture of Vietnam on the back, pointing out the location of Chu Lai. On the front were flags of both North and South Vietnam.

Don bought dolls for his sister and a jacket like mine for himself. It was great looking the place over.

Several children ran up asking, "Number One GI give me money?" And I was surprised at how good their English was.

We had been warned about giving them money. So we had no intention of doing so. Besides, I didn't have much left.

We also had been warned to watch the children that come up to us. It was a well-known fact that mothers would place bombs under their own children's clothes before sending them into the midst of other youngsters crowding around foreign soldiers. Then they'd pull the pin on the detonator, blowing you, themselves and everyone around them to parts unknown.

When we informed them no, they spat back, "You're Number Ten GI." And we knew this was the worst insult they could give a person. It seemed everything in this country was based on the number one to ten for quality.

After about three hours, we headed out, catching a ride all the way back, for which we were very thankful.

A few days later, I was told of a P.X. just down from the showers building. So I went to get a fan to help cool me off. I had electricity in my office, so that wasn't a problem.

I found it and though small, they had what I was looking for, so I bought the fan and took it back to the office. It worked so well, that except for a delivery of sandbags and one pick up of culvert, I spent the day in front of my fan.

At closing time, Sergeant Holt showed up and it was good to see him. I inquired, moving aside so he could share my fan, "How did the ambush go off?"

He replied, "It turned out to be a longer stay out than we anticipated. We just got in. I came right over to thank you. Those sandbags saved a lot of lives. Thank you from my men, too."

I asked, "Is there anything else your men need?"

Sergeant Holt remarked, "Nothing I can think of unless you have a few girls stashed in there with those sandbags." We both laughed and the conversation turned to just small talk.

When he left, I went to the Hooch where I found that the guys and their gear were gone. Locating Gary, in supply, he told me that they had all gone out on a mission several hours earlier. I thanked him and went back to the Hooch. It seemed more empty than usual and I hoped they wouldn't be gone long.

After supper, I found my name on the guard roster, so I cursed, "Damn, something else I wasn't looking forward to experiencing over here quite so soon."

But I wasn't all that surprised either with almost everyone in the company gone. Having nothing else to do, I hung around the Hooch until time to go.

When it came, we gathered in the waiting area with all our gear. I pretty well knew everyone by sight now and the Sergeant came out to give us our assignments. "Okay. In Bunker One, Melvin Dole, Danny Woods and Sal Wilson. Bunker Two, Sam Cook, Eddy Allen, and James Brown. Bunker Three Gary Walker, John Colburn, and Jessie Martinez. Bunker Four, Tim Cole, Ward Weaver, and Joe Jackson.

"Now, unless there're any questions, load up and let's get up that mountain before dark."

The road going up the mountain was so rough, it threw us around in the back of the truck. I was glad when we reached the top and stopped at the first Bunker. Dole, Woods, and Wilson got out taking an M-60 already in the truck, one for each Bunker, with them.

When we got out, Tim brought the 'Sixty out as the Sergeant told us, "Be ready when the truck gets here at 0600 or you walk down."

I entered the Bunker, looked around and saw it was a standard type of construction. Four by Four corner posts with Two by Twelves nailed outside these, making a solid wall. The front window was four and a half feet off the ground, with a three-foot high opening running the full width of the Bunker.

Against the outside walls and over the top of the ten by eighteen-foot structure lay three layers of sandbags.

Inside, the only things were the bunk beds along one wall. The door was in the side wall, toward the back.

I climbed on top to get a better look around, the sun had gone down, but it was still light enough to see as far as the terrain allowed out in front and to the horizon at the rear.

On both sides of us, every fifty meters or so, was another Bunker. The road we came upon ran behind the Bunkers.

Looking beyond the road, the mountain seemed to drop straight down. At the bottom of the drop was our company, with rows of other companies on both sides. Beyond that was the Air Base with the ocean beyond that. The whole thing looked like a picture.

Out in front of the Bunkers, where our attention would be for the night, was shrub brush about waist high for a couple hundred meters, then the timber line began.

As I looked the place over, I knew anyone could sneak up to within five meters or so from the Bunkers without being seen. We would have to be on extra alert on lookout. It all reminded me of my hunting grounds back home, which would be preferable to be at.

I called down to Joe, who seemed to know more of what was going on, "Couldn't we watch from up here, where it's cooler?"

Joe answered, "Everyone generally does. Stay up there and we'll hand everything up to you." And they did.

As we settled back, I noticed the Bunkers all had a length of cyclone fencing along the front of each one. The fencing was eight feet high to stop rockets from coming through the windows of the Bunkers.

I enjoyed the view until it was too dark to see further than a few meters out in front. So I brought my senses to full alert.

It was comfortable on top of the Bunker, with the light breeze blowing.

After a few hours, however, it got a little chilly. So I wrapped a blanket around myself that had been left behind.

Keeping our voices low, our talk was about back home. Joe was from Idaho; Tim, New York.

While Tim wasn't much of a talker, Joe and I held the conversation about home to low whispers. At least until Tim interrupted us with, "Who's on first watch?"

I spoke up, "I'm not sleepy, but how does it work?"

Joe explained, "One stays awake while the others sleep, changing every two hours or whatever is agreed upon."

Tim and Joe slept first while I watched the fireflies dancing gracefully to and fro. It was so beautiful all around us. The night went slow and, later, I took my turn sleeping.

The next morning, as the sun came up, we heard the trucks coming up the hill. One stopped at our Bunker, while the other continued on past us to stop at the next Bunker beyond ours.

By the time we were all packed up, no one had yet come out of the Bunker the other truck had stopped at. The driver of that truck got out and went inside the Bunker and as we loaded onto our truck, the guy came out of the Bunker and crawled on top of it as we headed back down the mountain.

Back in the Hooch, I showered before going to breakfast. Having the day off following guard duty, after eating I went down to the yard to let the workers have the day off as well.

As I approached my office, I noticed a large box sitting in front of my office door. I moved it aside with the edge of my boot, figuring whoever left it would be back soon to retrieve whatever it was.

Entering my office, I put my things on the desk and then brought the box in, placing it under my desk where it would be safer. Its contents were none of my business.

As I waited for the workers, my mind started working overtime. I'd heard of bombs being delivered this way. I wondered, 'could this box be a bomb?' I could deal with it, no matter the contents. But I had to know! There was apparently no one around to claim it, so I carefully picked it up and placed it on my desk.

Taking out my pocket knife, I slowly pushed the blade into the side of the box, close to the top and gently cut out a small hole about two inches square. After removing the piece, I looked in and saw the top of a bottle. Next, I slowly slipped my finger in the hole, feeling for wires, but there weren't any. I then cut a bigger hole and this time I saw the label on the bottle which read in big letters, "JACK DANIELS".

I sighed, opened the box by way of its top, and found four bottles of 86 proof whiskey in glass containers. I couldn't believe my eyes. You had to be a rank of Sergeant or above to buy whiskey in Vietnam and here I was in possession of four bottles! "WOW!" was all I could get out.

I closed the box, replaced it back under my desk, and sat down hoping some officer wasn't setting me up. That he wasn't just waiting for me to take it up to the Hooch and then bust me with them.

Right on time, the workers showed up and I informed them they didn't have to work today. So off they went, vanishing out of sight in no time at all.

I got ready to go, leaving the whiskey behind to deal with later, when a Vietnamese soldier in uniform showed up. Not recognizing his rank, I played it safe, asking, "Can I help you, Sir?"

He answered in very good English, "I hope so. You see, I need a few sandbags and can't get anyone to give them to me, not even with the paperwork. It seems we can be allies, but then it's made almost impossible for us to obtain the supplies we need. You're my last hope. I'll pay for any extra sandbags you have, as long as it doesn't short you or get you in trouble. "

I understood his dilemma, but asked, "Who are you?"

He extended a hand to shake mine: replying, "Excuse me, I'm Lieutenant Lee of the South Vietnamese Army."

As we shook hands, I went further, "I can't just give out sand-bags without paperwork, but where are you going anyway? If you can tell me."

"Wen Yu. You ever hear of it?"

It so happened that the day before I had read something about that place in the GI newspaper called "*The Stars and Stripes*". I now understood his plight. So I replied, "First off, I don't sell anything here. In my opinion, it's wrong. But I do have extra and because of where you're going, bring a couple men and I'll see what I can spare. I just hope it'll be enough."

Lieutenant Lee's face brightened as he smiled, saying, "Thank you. Whatever you give will be enough. I'll be right back." He grabbed my hand, shaking it violently, adding, "I'll be back in five minutes." And he rushed out the door and down the road. I watched him go, wondering how he was going to be back in five minutes. I hadn't heard of any Vietnamese units close by. I shrugged it off, for I liked the guy and felt I was doing the right thing as I settled down to wait.

I was snapped out of deep thought by a voice saying, "I'm

back." And looking, I saw Lieutenant Lee had two other Vietnamese soldiers with him.

I led them to the Conex and opened the door, instructing, "Have your men grab what they can carry," figuring they could deal with maybe one bundle apiece. But I was wrong as both guys picked up two bundles each, placed them on their shoulders as if they weighed nothing. I stood there in awe, but said nothing as they came out carrying the extra weight.

As I closed the doors, Lieutenant Lee thanked me again and then they were gone.

I wasn't tired anymore and wished the workers were back so we could do something. I just sat in front of my fan, keeping cool.

Half an hour later, the workers came back and were willing to work. We got some bundles of empty sandbags and shovels, then set to work filling the bags from a large sand dune between the lumber yard and Highway One. I wanted these for the new Bunker in the lumber yard and by noon, when I left to eat, we had a good start.

After lunch, I went back to the Hooch to pick up my weapon. Steve stuck his head in the door, saying, "Hey Weaver. The C.O. wants to see you on the double." And he was gone.

Wondering what was up, I gathered my gear, figuring to go directly from the C.O.'s office to the yard. I headed out, finding Cole and Jackson already there and the expression on their faces told me they had no more idea why we were there than I did.

The First Sergeant, sitting behind his desk, asked, "Did any of you see or hear anything out of the ordinary last night, or were you all sleeping, too?"

Joe spoke quickly, "We had a man awake at all times, just as required. If we had seen or heard anything, we would have called it in or reported it this morning. Why what happened?"

The First Sergeant replied, "In the Bunker next to yours, it was occupied by members of the First Company of the Sixth Infantry. If you didn't see or hear anything last night and were alert, this should make you want to be even more alert. Apparently, they went to sleep. This morning they were found on top of their Bunker, under poncho liners, dead with their throats cut!"

We looked at each other and I wondered if they were as scared as I suddenly was. I knew we had been alert and still hadn't seen or heard anything.

When we were dismissed, I went to work. The workers and I continued filling bags, but now stacking them against the Bunker.

Several days later, we had sandbags five layers wide laid against the sides and the same high over the top of the Bunker, giving it more protection than the others around had at their three layers.

Another week went by and I had forgotten all about Lieutenant Lee. Then he showed up one morning and as we shook hands, I said, "Glad to see you again, Sir. How, did your men do? "

He handed me a paper sack. I hadn't noticed him carrying as he told me, "This is my thanks to you. Please send it to someone you love back home."

I opened it, responding, "Thank you, but you really didn't have to." I couldn't imagine what it was until I pulled it from the sack. I was astonished beyond words. It was a black box about seven or so inches wide by about twenty inches long and approximately four inches high. On the lid, over the black paint, was a diorama of various colored flowers. It was so beautiful. I could tell it was well made and by hand. I inquired in surprise, "What's it made of?"

"Bamboo."

I opened the lid, finding a comb and brush made of the same material and there was a mirror attached to the inside of the lid. All I could think of to say was, "Thank you. It's so beautiful." He explained how the paints were made from different plant roots and that it was his way of thanking me.

I placed the box on my desk while Lieutenant Lee and I talked for the next half hour. Then he expressed "I have to go now. But I'll see you again soon." We shook hands and he left.

I sat at my desk, examining the box, fascinated by the workmanship someone had put into it. I knew I'd be sending it to my Mother as soon as possible.

The next day, another Sergeant came in and after some general conversation, he inquired, "What would be the chances of getting a few sandbags?"

"I sure would like to help. But I can't without a work order. Where are you and your men going?"

"Up on Hill 270 and I just wanted to take some with us in case."

I inquired casually, for I hadn't heard of this place. Of course, that didn't mean anything, there were a lot of places I hadn't heard about and never would. "Is it a Hot-Spot?" I had never been out on a mission, so the word "Hot-Spot" was just that, words.

I wondered further if I was unwillingly starting to play God. Like the bureaucrat's these guys had to deal with before finally coming to a place like mine, pleading for supplies. I hoped not, as he explained, "Not exactly. It's just that we take the hill, occupy it for a while, and then leave it. Only to go back a few months later to retake it again. It's a vicious cycle there." I thought this was the dumbest thing I had ever heard and told him so, getting a response of, "That's the Army way for you. So what can we do?"

I was beginning to learn, as I suggested, "How about I give you a bundle and you forget where you found it?"

He smiled nodding and after getting him one, he said, "I better be getting back. Thank you for the conversation and I hope whoever dropped this bundle knows how thankful we are." We shook hands and then he was gone and I knew that had been the right thing to do.

* * *

* * *

A knock on the door brought me out of my reverie. It was another Sergeant and I wondered why I was getting to be so popular. I opened the door and inquired, "Can I help you, Sergeant?" Knowing I could and would.

He replied, "I guess you get a lot of people trying to hit you up for materials and it must be getting tiresome?"

I exclaimed, "Naw, not really. If I don't feel they need them, I just say no if they haven't got the paperwork. I'm not trying to play God. But to some degree, I have to protect my job."

He spoke softly, "I'm Sergeant Taft and I guess I'm going to be one of those pests. Because I've come to ask for a favor, too. I can't discuss it, but if you could see fit to part with some sand-bags, any you could spare would be greatly appreciated."

I was going to tell him he had them, when he added, as if disgusted, "I guess we really don't need them. But one never knows what they're going to run into. We all go out with one thing in mind: Do the job the best we can, try to bring our men and us, or at least as many as possible, back alive as we can.

"People at S-1 and S-2 have never been out in the bush here and it's not like the other wars they were in..."

I raised a hand waving him off as I interrupted, "In my short time here, I've learned a lot and need to know more. I try to do what they tell me and still help out as many people as possible. Come and cool down in front of my fan." And I moved aside so he could feel the air from the fan as well.

He stepped directly in front of the fan, announcing, "Thank you. This does feel good. I'm sorry for getting carried away, but people in offices don't understand what we go through out there. They think we can do our job with just what we carry in our packs.

"I'm not a begging man, but if I thought it would do any good, I would." And he let out a sigh, watching the fan.

I could tell he had been wanting to say that for a long time. I told him, "You got as many sandbags as you want, whenever you come to pick them up, Sarge."

He went on as if not having heard me, "For the most part, we have enough men to do the job they ask us to do. If they would just let us do it without all the restrictions we have to follow. Rules the other side doesn't have to follow and materials can mean the difference. But the main Brass doesn't care about lives.

"You've heard their slogan, 'Ours is not to reason why, but to do or die'? Well, with that kind of reasoning, what can you expect from them?" He stopped abruptly, going into deep thought. Then looking at me, he inquired, "Did you say I could have the bags?"

I told him, nodding, "Now and any time you need them. But I would like to learn all I can about out there. But not the hard way by going out. So please, get your men and, afterward, maybe you'll help me understand more?"

Sergeant Taft said kind of apologetically, "I didn't mean to talk you into something, I get carried away some ..."

I interrupted, "I won't let myself get into trouble. So don't worry, I have extras put away and you can help me have a better ability to know how to use them." He exclaimed, "Thanks, I'll be right back." And getting up to leave, he added, "And we will talk," then he was gone.

I sat pondering what he had told me, knowing the guy wasn't begging, nor asking for sympathy. What he said held meaning for me and I wanted to learn more.

I was still in thought when Sergeant Taft knocked on the door, accompanied by four other men. I led them to the far Conex where I opened the door and announced, "Take what you need."

Sergeant Taft responded, "Thank you." Then his men got two bundles each and then followed the Sergeant and me back to the office where the Sergeant sent his men on ahead and we sat in front of the fan, talking for the next hour.

The next few weeks went by normally, until one night after supper, I found myself on the Guard Duty roster again. So, in disgust, I got my gear and was assigned a Bunker.

I pulled guard with Phil Saddler and Tim Collins this time. After we were dropped off at the Bunker, without even going inside, we took ourselves and equipment up on top of the Bunker.

As we settled down, I said, "I never checked inside this bunker. Did either of you?"

Phil and Tim looked at each other for a second before Tim grabbed his M-16, jumped off the Bunker and vanished inside.

A second later he emerged, climbing back up to join us.

"It's clear inside," he said.

We were sharing small talk when the landline phone rang and I answered it, being the closest. "Private Weaver, Bunker two,"

I said into the mouthpiece.

After all the Bunkers reported on line, a voice said, "This is

Lieutenant Lincoln and I'm informing all Bunkers we're on Yellow Alert. Intelligence says we could get hit by up to two thousand Vietnamese. So no sleeping and stay alert. That's all." And everyone hung up.

I looked out front of the Bunker as thoughts raced through my head. Not for long though, as Phil broke in, "What's wrong, Weaver? You see something out there?"

"No," I answered. Then I explained what the Lieutenant had said, finishing with, "Let's move everything inside for tonight?" And without further comment, everyone set to work, and in hardly no time, we had everything set up in the window inside.

We were silent for a while. Then I asked Phil, since he had been there much longer than me, he may know, "Say, Phil, how is Intelligence able to tell how many or even approximately how many Vietnamese we're going to be hit by? I'm sure the VC don't call us giving out that kind of information."

Phil replied, "Old Charlie leaves a calling card before striking. You see, Old Charlie believes that as long as his coffin is built, he goes to Heaven whether he gets put in it or not after death. So he builds his own coffin and leaves them in the woods.

"When one of our patrols run across a pile of coffins, all they have to do is count the coffins piled up and they know how many are going to hit us in the next day or so." I inquired, "How accurate is the count?"

"It's generally within a few bodies, but accurate enough." There was no more talk as we stood transfixed, looking out the window before us as time seemed to stand still.

The sound of an engine coming up behind our Bunker caused me to rush out as a jeep stopped in front of me. Its passenger handed me an object about fourteen inches long and maybe four or five inches in diameter. Then the guy informed me, "This will be part of every Bunkers' equipment from now on."

I replied, a little puzzled, "Okay, but what is it?"

He answered, "A Star-Light Scope;" And the driver drove off toward the next Bunker.

I re-entered the Bunker and Phil asked, "What did they want?"

I told him, "They gave me something called a Star-Light Scope. Whatever the hell that is? I wonder what it does."

Phil spoke excitedly, taking the Scope from me, "They're great, and you know what infrared is, don't you?"

I replied, "Yeah, I do."

He continued, "Well, as you know if you have an Infrared Scope and so does the enemy, you can detect each other's rays. But if you both have a Star-Light, neither can detect the other.

"But now here is where it gets good, if we have the Star-Light and the enemy has Infrared, we can detect them, but not the other way around.

"Another thing, as you know, infrared makes everything look red, whereas the Star-Light makes it all green. I've taken the caps off, so have a look and see." And he handed it to me.

I took a look and saw that it made things a little green, as well as almost natural day-like, and clear, too. I kind of hogged it for the next few hours, like a kid with a new toy.

About midnight, I was again looking through the scope when I heard a noise out front and thought I saw the brush moving in an unnatural manner. I asked the others not taking my eye from the Scope, "Did you hear that?"

Tim didn't respond, but Phil did, "I think so."

About then, there was another noise and this time whatever it was, wasn't trying to be quiet. But I couldn't find it in the Scope and didn't want us shooting without a target. I also didn't want to wait until it was right in front of the Bunker before reacting, when it could be too late.

I was getting right down apprehensive about the situation when I decided to get permission to act. I picked up the phone, turned the little crank on the side and a voice asked, "What do you need?" Before I could answer, I heard receivers being picked up from other Bunkers, too.

I said, "Weaver here in Bunker Two. Someone's pushing through the brush out in front of us, not caring about being quiet. We don't want to shoot and give our position away. Nor do we have a visual. We'd like permission to use a grenade?"

The voice asked, "Could it be an animal?"

I answered, "I thought of that. But the movement I did see, if it's an animal, it's a tall one!" I wasn't sure if I had lied about that last part, but my imagination was really running wild as I waited.

Soon the voice replied, "If you think it's something other than an animal, permission granted and all the rest of the Bunkers, you know what's going on, so be alert! It could be what we've been waiting for! Good luck." And each Bunker responded before everyone hung up.

I picked up a grenade as I walked to the door. I pulled the pin, holding the handle against the grenade. Then I told the others, "Tim, get on the 'Sixty and Phil watch through the scope."

I then released the handle of the grenade, stepped outside as the handle popped off the grenade, and counted to three.

Then I threw it before I slipped back inside and rushed to the window picking up my rifle and was ready when the grenade went off.

When it did, I strained my eyes looking for any kind of movement now, but there wasn't any. Yet we waited.

After about ten minutes, I asked, "Anyone see anything?"

As they both said they hadn't, the phone rang and I answered it reluctantly, "Bunker two, Weaver here."

After the other Bunkers reported on line, a voice asked, "Is everything okay up there?"

Knowing it was aimed at me, I answered, "Nothing yet."

The voice warned, "Stay alert and if you think something out there isn't an animal, use another grenade!"

The night crawled along very slowly, but nothing happened, and there was no talking either for the rest of the night.

Morning came, not any too soon for me, and before our truck arrived, I checked out the bush where the grenade went off. I found nothing. So when the truck got there, we loaded on and I expected joking to be poked at me over what I'd done. I was surprised when there wasn't any.

The squad came in from the field later and that night Don and I went to the movie and then the club for a few beers. Before retiring, Don announced, "Don't anyone wake me in the morning." And we all went to sleep.

The next morning, when I went to the office, I found another box. It was much larger than the first one and heavier when I shoved it aside with my foot.

I placed my things inside before bringing the box in, but this time, I placed in on the desk. When I inspected the box, I

54

found printed in big letters "SP" on all four sides and wondered what they meant.

I could hardly wait to see what was in this one, for I knew it wasn't whiskey. I carefully opened it and found several cartons of cigarettes inside. Two cartons of Salem's, two were Pall Mall, one was a carton of Marlboro, and the last two were Camels.

I also found several pencils and sheets of unlined paper, two boxes of Snicker candy bars, two boxes of Mars bars, one box of Hersheys, and a box of Tropical bars. The latter of which I had never heard of. But I figured to find out later what they tasted like.

There were even several boxes of Lifesavers candy and five books of various stories. That was the total contents of the box. I loaded everything back into it and placed it under the desk with the whiskey and started working on my ledger.

I got in two loads, one of culvert pipe and the other was landing mat.

After lunch, a runner came in saying the CO wanted ten doors made. He gave me the paper with the dimensions, then left.

I didn't have any screen material, nor did I know how to order supplies through regular channels. So I wrote a note, addressed it to S-1, asking how to place these orders, then signed it and put it in my pocket.

Just as I was getting ready to close and let the workers go, a truck pulled into the yard. It was as if someone was reading my mind. The truck contained ninety-six rolls of screen. We quickly unloaded everything, placing them inside the office so they could be put away in the morning.

The next day, I decided it was time to get a haircut. After

lunch, I inquired, "Where's the Barber Shop around here? I think it's about time to get a haircut."

Mike informed me, "Toward the mountain up from the shower. But it's not safe going there alone."

"Why?" I asked, figuring I was a big boy and could take care of myself. Surely, I didn't need a chaperone to get a haircut.

Mike announced, "I need a haircut, too. So I'll go with you. A while back, a Lieutenant and a Captain, separately, found out the hard way why you don't go there alone. Both had their throats cut by the Barber! It's a Vietnamese that cuts our hair here in the Barber Shop."

I asked, very puzzled as we got our gear heading for the door, "Why are they allowed to cut hair if this goes on?"

Mike shrugged, answering, "Cheap labor, I guess." And we were on our way.

On the way, we swung by S-1, and I dropped off the paper in my pocket and the monthly reports.

At the Barber Shop, there was a male Vietnamese wearing a white apron. I looked at Mike, who told me, "You first." As he injected a round into the chamber of his M-16.

I sat down in the chair telling the barber to give me a butch haircut and he began cutting.

It didn't take long for him to finish and after brushing me off, Mike got in the chair asking for the same haircut. I injected a round into my weapon, wondering how I would react if the barber cut Mike's throat? Oh, there was no doubt I would kill him. But would it be in time to save Mike's life?

I was relieved when Mike was finished and we were on our way back to the Hooch and a shower.

That evening, I was sitting in the Hooch alone when Cole and Don came in one door of the Hooch as Mike, Paul, and John came in the other. I commented jokingly, "Christ, I'm being invaded from both sides."

The five of them laughed as Don remarked, "We should. The way you sit down in the lumber yard all day, doing nothing."

Knowing he was joking, I smarted back, "Then I'll just keep what I've obtained for you, sitting on my ass all day."

Don responded bringing laughter from the others, "What, a box of shit?"

I came back with, "Maybe. But I think you're going to like and want this box of shit!"And they all looked at me seriously as I smiled at them.

Now Don responded, "Okay, you've got our curiosity going now."

Having prepared for this, I had previously brought both boxes up earlier, stashing them under my cot, and letting my blankets hang over the sides, hiding between them. I went to my cot and pulled the smaller one out, placed it on the table and told them, "Open this and see."

Don opened the box quickly as the others looked over his shoulder. I stood back, giving them room.

When it was seen what the box contained, they all sounded off in unison, "WOW!" Then Don asked, still in surprise, "Where did you get these, buddy?"

I informed them all loudly, "I'll never talk. You can torture me... Well, if you do a little, I'll talk. "And they all laughed as the bottles were removed from the box and I told them, "The truth is, I couldn't tell you if I wanted,"

John interrupted, "You mean they just appeared?"

I told them seriously, "That's exactly what happened."

After a little skepticism from some of the guys, I explained how I came by the boxes, finishing with, "So shall we get some beer and really have a party?"

Paul spoke up, "Okay, everyone, ante up so we can make this a party to remember." As they dug money from their pockets. I started to give what little I had when Paul told me, "You donated the whiskey. For now, we'll take care of the beer."

Cole and Don were elected to go for the beer and they each returned carrying three cases of Ballantine Beer and the party got started.

We proceeded to get drunk as guys from other buildings soon joined our party and, surprisingly, it was after midnight before we ran out of booze and money, even mine.

Once everyone, except for those of us that lived there cleared out, Mike started running through the empty cans and bottles asking loudly, "Who's hiding the booze?"

We all looked at each other and I finally told Mike, "It's all gone, Mike. It was one hell of a party, but now it's over, and it's bedtime." And I laid on my cot, because the room wouldn't stop moving of its own accord.

Mike started sounding mean, throwing cans and bottles around shouting, "If someone doesn't bring out the booze they're hiding, I'm going to tear this place apart!"

The room was really spinning for me now as I heard Sam ask, "What're we going to do? The last time it took all of us to take him down, and we weren't drunk like we are now!"

When no one answered, I suddenly remembered something

my father bragged about doing once. Gathering my strength, I got off the bed, I grabbed a chair to steady myself and said, "He's got us, fellows." Then I directed my words to Mike, "You're right, Mike. But we're going to get it for you right now." And I staggered out the door with several of the guys behind me.

Outside, John inquired, "What've you got in mind, Ward?

Sam added before I could speak, "Yah, for Mike's about to tear the Hooch and us up real good."

Being drunk as I was and the thought of what I had in mind, I couldn't help laughing as the others waited.

When I was able to control myself, I explained, "My father once told me about feeding a drunk piss to sober him, and it worked. What have we got to lose?"

Paul interjected, "Our lives, if he realizes what he's drinking. We could all die tonight." And I knew he was probably right.

Someone presented a whiskey bottle which we all took turns pissing in, and when no one could go anymore, I took the bottle. "We can't give it to him this warm," I said, "He'll..."

John interrupted, rushing off, "I'll be right back."

I didn't know how long he was gone, but he returned with a bag of ice. We put a lot of ice inside the bottle and capped it. I shook it until the ice dissolved, according to what we could see when someone lit his lighter.

Satisfied it was cool enough, we entered the Hooch and I handed the bottle to Mike who was sitting on his bed. I said, "Sorry it took so long, but we forgot where it had been put."

Mike snatched the bottle saying with scorn, "I'll bet there was more, but you guys just didn't want to share with me! So I'm not sharing any of this with any of you!" And he opened the bottle, taking a long drink of the liquid as the rest of us held our breath, waiting to see what his reaction was going to be.

When Mike parted his mouth from the bottle, he belched before exclaiming, "Damn, this is warm."

In my drunken state, all I could think to say, knowing the others were breathing a little easier, just as I was, "Isn't it everywhere?"

I didn't wait to watch him finish. I just laid on my cot, closing my eyes, I welcomed sleep, and an end to this night.

I woke to an explosion and someone yelling, "INCOMING!"

I jumped from my cot as the Hooch came alive. Mike's actions were as if nothing had happened and by the next explosion, we were all heading out the door.

I could still feel the effects of the booze, but it seemed like no one else was. But by the time we reached the Bunker, I had lost track of how many explosions had gone off. However, all hell seemed to have broken loose and, from inside the Bunker, it was hard to keep track of where they were all landing.

After half an hour, the bombardment of mortars stopped as quickly as they had started and all was quiet. Still, no one talked. We just kept watching for movement of any Vietnamese coming from the perimeter.

Suddenly, it sounded as if all the Bunkers on the mountain opened up with everything they had. I got this vision of being overrun, like in the movies, and felt fear as the sky brightly lit up all along the ridge of the mountain by flares.

A voice from the door of the Bunker shouted, "Three men stay put! The rest spread out! We're in Code Red!"

I came out of our Bunker quickly making my way down the hill to the lumber yard. At my Bunker, I found two guys already occupying it. I took up a position at the window beside them.

Seconds, before I heard them, one of the guys, announced, "Here come the gunships." And then I could hear them coming.

We rushed outside as they came up from behind us maybe fifty feet off the ground. Four beautiful gunships. They flew over us, heading for the mountain.

Stopping, they just hovered below the rim of the mountain. Then after a few minutes, staying abreast of each other, they quickly rose above the ridge. They lifted their tails even higher, almost standing on their nose. Then they suddenly opened fire with all their weapons.

Even though there were five rounds of regular ammunition between red tracer rounds, it looked like several solid red lines connecting the gunships to the ground. It was a picture worth framing, but I didn't have my camera.

A few seconds of this and the four gunships dropped suddenly below the rim of the mountain as green tracers from the ground beyond the bunkers on the mountains filled the sky where the gunships had been.

The choppers didn't hover long before rising quickly and repeated the action of their first round. But now red and green tracers seemed to fill the same space.

As four gunships hovered again below the rim of the mountain, I didn't see the other two gunships approaching. But when they placed themselves on each side of the current gunships, I could see these two looked different from the other helicopter gunships. They were more streamlined and menacing looking, but still beautifully sleek. Not taking my eyes off them, I asked, "What are those?"

"Cobras! Now watch the fun." Someone answered as we waited for the new show to start.

In unison, all six jumped above the ridge and Bunkers, along with green and red tracers filling the sky. Flames trailing the rockets fired from the two new gunships streaked across the sky to the ground quickly finding their targets.

After a few seconds of this, the six gunships sank below the rim to hover for a while before they rose to do it all over again.

This went on for the better part of half an hour when everything fell quiet, and we watched the gunships turn, heading back to the airbase. I didn't turn away from watching them until they were out of sight.

Looking back at the mountain, there were two gunships I hadn't seen before. They were hovering approximately in the same place the others had been. They looked like the two the guy had called Cobras.

They both slowly rose above the mountain and Bunkers, but no one fired. Even the Bunkers were quiet with no green tracers from the ground stirring the air as the Cobras moved forward over the top of the mountain and Bunkers.

Flares still lit the sky and soon green tracers flew past one of the slow-moving Cobras. The other raised its tail and opened up with machine guns as well as rockets at the area from which the green tracers had come.

When the green tracers stopped, the gunship leveled off, but it continued hovering as the other one slowly moved off. It was becoming evident that it was drawing fire for the other.

This went on for the next half hour, drawing green tracers two more times. Then for the next twenty minutes nothing happened. So the two gunships left and the flares died down to a few here and there being set off and lighting small areas.

We went back inside the Bunker and at the window, I asked casually, "Well that's over. I wonder if they'll let us go back to bed now."

It was too dark to see who answered and I hadn't thought to see who I was sharing the Bunker with when it was well lit up. "Don't know, it's already 0500."

Daylight came quickly, and I didn't know the guys with me in the Bunker, so when a whistle blew, we all headed in our own directions.

Back in the Hooch, everyone put their gear away and cleaned up before going to breakfast. There wasn't time to take a nap, though I really wanted one badly.

Don asked me as we ate, "Where were you last night? Paying more attention to the fireworks than where you were going?"

He chuckled, delaying his taking another bite of his food as I had to admit he was partially right. I told him of my flight to the lumber yard and finding the two guys there. Then he told me about ending up in a Bunker near the shower building.

When the workers showed up, Joe asked, "We going to build the doors today?"

I responded, not feeling like doing anything, but sleep, "Not this morning. Maybe later. Just hang around and if you see anyone coming, knock on the wall of my office before they get here. I'm going to take a nap."

He agreed to and I locked the door, then laid my head on the desk and closed my eyes.

It only seemed like seconds passed when there was a knock on the wall. I looked and saw the company runner coming. I unlocked the door and opening it, inquired as he arrived, "I hope they don't want those doors today. I won't be getting to them until at least tomorrow."

He replied, handing me an envelope, "No, just delivering this." Then he turned and left in the direction he came.

It contained two letters. The first telling me my Supply Office had the paperwork I needed for making orders for supplies I needed. The other informed me of my advance in rank to Specialist Fourth Class.

This was what I needed to wipe the tiredness from my eyes and mind. I left the office, heading for Supply. I was greeted by Gary, who asked, "What can I do for you today, Ward?"

"I need a stack of forms, to order Supplies. I also need a couple sets of Specialist Fourth Class stripes, I got my promotion."

"Congratulations. What kind do you want? The kind for sewing on your sleeve or the type that pin on your collar?"

After a moment of consideration, I told him, "Why not a few of each?"

Nodding, he got them for me, along with the forms I'd requested. I thanked him and headed for the Hooch, where I removed the stripes from my shirt sleeve and placed the pin type to my collar. The rest I could put on later. I went to work, and we started working on making the doors.

That Saturday, I decided to take off. When Don and the squad came in early, accompanied by a new guy. Don introduced him to me, "Hey, Ward. This is Rebel. He just got assigned to our squad. Why don't you take the day off and we'll take him to the village?"

I shook Rebel's hand, saying, "Hi. Glad you're with us." Then I told Don, "Going to the village sounds like a great idea. When would you two like to leave?"

Rebel suggested before Don could answer, "Let's go now?" Don agreed, so we gathered our gear and headed for the front gate.

We were lucky, catching a ride not far down Highway One, all the way to the village limits.

Don and I injected a round into the chamber of our rifles, telling Rebel to do the same.

As he did, Don and I slung our rifles, took out a hand grenade each and holding the handle against it firmly, we pulled the pins, and Rebel inquired, "What're you doing that for?"

Don explained as we walked into the village, "This is how you go into a village. Just don't let go of the handle unless you plan to throw it! No one will bother us this way, and later you just put the pin back in and off you go. No fuss, no muss."

Rebel shrugged, took a grenade, copied us and then asked, "There's got to be more to why we're doing this than that."

I spoke now, "It's like this. Several things can happen in a village. We just want to prevent them from happening to us! You see life is expendable to these people. It's not uncommon for someone to ..." I pointed at the children off to one side and continued, "Take one of them, strap a bomb to them under their clothes before sending them to us for candy. Get the point?" I stopped for a moment before finishing with, "There are a lot of VC, sympathizers in these villages."

We bought a few things before I heard Rebel ask Don real low, "Ward was joking, wasn't he? That's just propaganda . . ."

Don interrupted, "Rebel, I hope you never have to find out. But be assured that many G.I.'s have died finding out too late. "

We walked on and now Rebel seemed to be more aware of the dangers around him and us.

The girls in every doorway tried to entice all GI's into their homes by calling out, "Number One G.I. want Bookoo Boom Boom? Number One Girl here." And they all caught Rebel's eye.

Don told Rebel, catching him staring at one in particular, "Go for it, they only charge five dollars a trick." Don and I laughed when Rebel walked on as if disgusted with us.

Almost through the village, Rebel stopped abruptly. Don and I looked to see what had suddenly captured Rebel's attention. It was a very beautiful woman. One look told you she was half French and half-Vietnamese, due to her tall stature.

As we stood there, Rebel didn't take his eyes from her and said, "Excuse me boys, but I've been given an invitation I can't refuse."

I responded, "I don't blame you. Go ahead and enjoy, we'll wait for you here." And we watched as Rebel and the girl vanished inside the house. If you wanted to call them houses, that is. They were made of car body parts, plywood, lumber, and tin. They had doorways, but no doors; window frames, but no glass. There was just pieces of cloth hanging in them, acting as such, and the floor was the ground.

I looked at Don and exclaimed, "Damn, you ever see one more beautiful than that one?"

"Not lately. WOW!"

We stood there now in the middle of the road, looking around. If Don's thoughts paralleled mine, he was thinking about getting one of these girls too, for I surely was.

We watched the Vietnamese doing their shopping and G.I.'s buying things. I don't know how much time passed, when there was an explosion from either in or behind the house Rebel had entered.

Don and I hit the ground, our rifles off our shoulders and in one hand, the grenade still in the other. We scanned the area and everyone was on the ground, villagers, and GI's alike.

The longer we waited, the harder my heart seemed to pound.

Then Rebel emerged from the house, announcing, "Sorry everyone, everything's okay." Everyone slowly got up and soon movement in the village was as if nothing had happened.

Don and I went to Rebel who was smiling and Don inquired a little irritated, "What the hell happened?"

Snickering, Rebel began, "You are not going to believe . . ."

I interrupted, a little angry myself, "Try us and it better be good. I'm not in the mood for jokes right now."

Rebel got serious after looking into my face and explained, "Well, you see I was banging that beautiful girl in there and it was feeling fantastic. She's quite talented, you know..."

I pointed my weapon at his head, breaking in, "I want to know about the explosion, not what her abilities are. Now get to it. "

As I lowered my rifle, he continued, "Well I forgot having the grenade in my hand and... and... well, I didn't really..."

Don now cut him off, "Just tell us what happened."

Rebel swallowed hard and did. "Well, the fact is that when I climaxed, I accidentally dropped it..., well, I didn't want to stop. So I scooped it up and threw it out the window as far as I could in that position. I just hoped for the best and finished what I was doing. And that's what happened."

Don and I looked at each other in disbelief. Then we walked past Rebel, entered the house to check out his story. We found the girl, still lying as petrified as Rebel had left her. She didn't even move or try to cover her nakedness when we came in. She just laid there watching us, moving only her eyes.

The smell of gunpowder was strong and most of the back wall was gone. It had apparently been blown inward, so turning to Rebel I asked, "How the hell did you live through this or keep from getting hit by shrapnel? You both look okay. But you should have been killed. Are you part cat?"

Rebel answered, "I don't know. We just laid there and I felt the blast, but that's all."

Don and I shook our heads in amazement before Don told Rebel, "You are without a doubt one lucky son-of-a-bitch. We better get out of here." So we left, agreeing not to talk about this again because no one would believe it anyway.

We decided to call it a day and headed out. We got lucky again and caught a jeep going through the village and rode to the company in silence.

That night I wrote a letter home telling mom about all the events since my last letter.

The next few days were routine. Loads came in and went out. Then one evening after supper, Sergeant Hicks came in announcing, "We move out in the morning, early men. So get your gear together. Draw supplies and get some rest." Then he looked at me inquiring, "And how's the lumber business working out? Tired of it yet?"

"No." I replied and after a pause added, "It's going really well down there, Sergeant. No complaints."

He just nodded and left as the guys started putting their gear together. Gary opened the supply room, so everyone got what they needed. Then we all settled down for the night.

I laid there in the dark looking up into nothing waiting for sleep to overtake me when like a jolt, I remembered the SP package. I jumped from my bed, turned on the light, and then called out as a few shouted for me to turn off the light, "Come here first everyone, I almost forgot something I have for you all. It may be too late in the morning to do it."

They all got up, coming to the table as I retrieved the box from under my bed. I placed it on the table as a few grumbled until the box was opened. Then all I heard was, "WOW!" And I knew they had forgotten all about sleep and being tired.

It was Paul who spoke first, "Where'd you get this..."

Don interrupted, "He told you. The same way he got the whiskey that we polished off."

Paul nodded, remembering as I said, "Take what you want." As I unloaded the box, they took what they wanted, stashing it in their packs.

As we crawled back in bed and the lights were turned out, everyone thanked me again. Soon we were all sound asleep.

I woke the next morning, alone in the Hooch and said a silent good luck as my gut told me this one was more than routine.

That night I had to pull Guard Duty. So after supper, I fell out with full gear, ready to go up the mountain.

A new Sergeant came out and announced, "My name is Sergeant Baker and tonight, rather than going up the mountain, we've been assigned to guard the Bong Song Bridge. For those of you who have never been there, a Bunker is at each end of the bridge. It should be an easy night."

"And before there are any questions, we guard it because it's a crucial bridge on Highway One. Charlie drifts explosives down the river at night blowing it up and then we spend the next day rebuilding it. Your job is to spot someone floating anything down the river and blow it up before it gets to the bridge.

"Each of you will be given a box of tracers for this purpose. Just fill one clip. Any questions?" There wasn't any.

We were each given a box of tracers and as we loaded a clip, Sergeant Baker read from his clipboard, "Okay then, on the South side of the bridge will be Paul Johnson, Brad Jennings, Tim Cook, Sal Wilson, and Eddy Allen." I wondered if this Cook was any relation to Don. The Sergeant now continued, "On the North side will be Cole Black, Ward Weaver, Joe Jackson, John Smith, and Paul Logan. Now load up."

We climbed into the back of a pick-up truck, while the Sergeant climbed in front to ride shotgun.

The ride was nice with little talk. I enjoyed the scenery along the way, seeing people working the rice fields as others traveled in both directions on the Highway. The ones in the field interested me the most. But I wondered why they wore their baggy clothes in the watery fields.

I got my answer when the truck stopped long enough to let a Water Buffalo be herded across the road before us.

As I watched the people in the field, one of the women about twenty meters from our truck, stopped in the middle of her work. She gathered up the loose left pants' leg and raised it. Then pulling it aside, she revealed she wasn't wearing panties. She squatted and proceeded to relieve herself in the rice paddy in full view of everyone.

I must have had my mouth open in astonishment. For it wasn't long before one of the guys nudged me, saying, "That's why they wear them so baggy and they aren't shy as you can see. Matter of fact, she won't even wipe herself when she's finished. "

I watched in doubt, but sure enough as soon as she was finished, the woman just stood, releasing her pants leg, which fell down covering her and she walked on as if nothing had happened. At that moment, though, we drove on.

When we reached the bridge, I looked around from the back of the truck. This place could easily pass for a number of places on the river back home.

I got off the truck because this was our Bunker.

The truck drove across the bridge as I noticed that beyond the Bunker on the other side of the bridge was a village.

Also, I quickly noticed there were two bridges running parallel to each other across the river. One was a floating bridge. The other was a steel expanding bridge some thirty meters above the water. The truck was crossing the latter one as I watched.

The area to the east and west of us was a little hilly in the distance. In the immediate area, it was mostly flat.

I saw the truck return after it dropped the others off. The Sergeant gave us a thumbs up as they drove past.

I went into the Bunker and laid my gear on the top bunk bed.

I kept my weapon and clip with tracers and went back outside and began looking around the area, trying to get a better feel of it for after it got dark. I saw Cole standing off by himself, while the others were together in a group talking. Their gear was lying near the Bunker door. So I went to Cole, who was still carrying all of his gear and asked, "Why don't you dump your gear like the rest and get comfortable?"

He nodded, walked towards the Bunker and vanished inside. He soon emerged a few seconds later still wearing his pistol belt containing ammunition pouches and bayonet. I asked, pointing at his belt, "Why are you still wearing that?"

He patted the bayonet and answered, "Security blanket."

I just shrugged, turned to the others, and heard Joe ask, "What are we going to do while we wait for dark?"

I spoke up first, "There's really nothing to do." And knew it would be dark soon anyway. I watched the number of people walking up and down Highway One getting fewer and fewer, knowing anyone walking on it after dark would be shot by us as VC.

Suddenly Joe called to an old man, "Hey Popason. Come here a moment." And Joe motioned for the old Vietnamese guy to come over to us.

The old man came, but stopped a few feet away from Joe, who asked the old man, "You know Number One Girl for us, Popason?"

The old man smiled, responding, "Oh yes, Number One Babyson. Own daughter, Number One Girl. You like me to get for you? "

Joe replied, "You bet Popason, if she Number One, we all are going to want her. You think Babyson can handle all of us? "

Smiling even bigger, the old man answered, "Oh yes. Daughter handle real good. I go get her, right now." And he rushed off as fast as his short legs would carry him across the bridge.

Soon only a silhouette gave him away in the dim-lit sky.

I asked of no one in particular, "I wonder if she really is his daughter?"

John announced, "I don't know, nor do I care, as long as she's young. Of course, if she is, it's right generous of the old man."

Joe spoke now, "She probably is. They're so money hungry over here, and life is so meaningless. If a daughter can bring in some money, they don't care how it happens or by what means." Then he turned to John asking, "Hey remember what happened to ol' Sergeant Bail?"

John nodded, then started shaking his head at the memory. Joe just kept looking at us, explaining, "He paid this Babyson her five dollars and went to bed with her. He shoved himself inside her body, only to pull himself out quicker than he went in. He got more than he bargained for because he then had four small ones." He and John now started snickering.

I didn't know if I was the only one that didn't get it as I commented, "That doesn't make sense."

This caused John and Joe to laugh hard and the others seemed to mock me, joining in on the laughter. John finally told me, "Oh, don't mind them, it could happen to any ..."

Joe quickly interrupted, "Like hell, I make em stick their own finger up inside themselves to make sure they don't have any damn razor blades up inside there."

I thought he was joking, even though he sounded serious. So I kind of demanded, "Explain, for you're either joking," sounding serious, "or when I see them coming, I'll blow 'em away before they get off the bridge!"

I think everyone thought I was joking now as they all laughed, except for Joe, who told me, "Sometimes these girls try to kill us with sex. They've been known to break the neck off a bottle or put razors in a cork and then shove either one up inside themselves. When a GI shoves his tool up inside her, the glass peels the skin off or the razor blades cut him down the middle.

"But in Sergeant Bail's case, the girl had two razor blades criss-crossed in cork. Get the picture now?"

A chill ran down my spine picturing this. I inquired, "Then how do you know who you can and can't have sex with?"

Joe told me, "Don't worry, they only do it when there's just one GI. They're not stupid enough to do it in a situation like this."

I was in deep thought when Paul said, "Here they come."

I wondered how he could know that. It was too dark to see very far with the moon just coming out. I asked, "How do you know they're coming?"

Paul replied, "I called the other side to let them pass and I still have them on the line. The old man and a girl just went past their Bunker, heading this way." I hadn't seen him go in the Bunker and bring out the line phone.

A few seconds went by and then I saw two silhouettes coming off the bridge.

When they got to us, the moon only revealed that the girl was very petite with long hair.

The old man spoke first, "Number One daughter. You like?" Joe responded, "Yeah, we like very much."

The old man then said, "Five American Dollars each, please."

Joe declared, digging into his pocket, "I'm first! If there's no objection because I got her here." There wasn't.

Joe paid and took the girl's hand leading her into the Bunker, as the old man waited outside with us.

As we waited, I heard John and Paul talking about who would be next. I wasn't sure if I even wanted a turn after what I had learned tonight.

Cole asked, "Aren't we supposed to be watching the river?"

I figured if the other Bunker wasn't doing the same thing we were, they could watch the river. However, I figured they were probably doing the exact same thing, being at the edge of the village. So I told Cole, "We are, it just doesn't look like it to you. You're on watch first and when Joe comes out, he'll take your place."

"Okay," he replied, walking off.

After what seemed long enough for Joe to have done half a dozen girls, John called in to him, "Hey Joe, how much more time do you need?"

Joe called back, "I've been finished with her for some time now, but she won't let go. I think she's in love. I have that effect on women. I really should have gone last." And we could hear him laughing and we joined his laughter, entering the pitch black Bunker.

The four of us and Popason made our way to the bunk bed and I lit my lighter inside my helmet. The light revealed Joe lying there with the girl's arms wrapped tightly around his neck. Her face buried against his shoulder. It was obvious she was hanging on for dear life and Joe was definitely enjoying himself.

John told the girl, "Come on, bitch. Give the rest of us a turn." And he reached over taking hold of her arm and pulled. But she just tightened her arms around Joe's neck.

My lighter got hot, so I put it out. Paul struck a match, holding it in his helmet and I saw John kick the girl in her bare ass. The girl flinched, but said nothing, nor did she move.

The match didn't last long and when it went out, Paul asked, "What shall we do now?"

John answered, "Let the old man deal with her." Another match was lit as John turned to the old man exclaiming, "She Number Ten daughter Popason. She's a bitch. What are you going to do about this?"

The match went out as the old man started talking angrily at the girl. I couldn't make out any of what he was saying. I didn't figure it was nice, though. But the girl just ignored him.

Another match was lit, the old man walked up to Cole and before anyone knew what had happened, the old man moved like a cat and in the blink of an eye, reached out snatching Cole's bayonet from its scabbard. Then he turned, heading back for the bunk as someone shouted, "LOOK OUT!"

The match went out as I quickly brought my rifle from being slung on my shoulder, figuring everyone else was doing the same. Then I waited, it being too dark to see a target.

Paul quickly lit his lighter and it revealed all weapons trained on the old man beside the bunk as he reached down filling his free hand with the girl's hair and pulling back hard as he could, John quickly said, "Easy everyone. He's not after Joe."

We could see that Joe no longer thought this was funny. He was watching Popason while trying to back away from the girl, but the wall prevented his escape.

The girl just seemed to tighten her hold on Joe's neck, the harder Popason pulled on her hair. In a flash, with the girl's head back over her shoulders, the knife flashed around in front of the girl's throat and in one movement, the old man cut her throat from one side to the other.

The match went out as we heard the gurgling sound coming from the girl as she died. I was frozen like a statue, my mind was a blank, except for the last scene I saw.

Even though it was pitch black, I swore I could see the old man turn and move toward one of the guys, then stop in front of him. But my mind wouldn't function to form thoughts, words, or action. This guy had just killed his own daughter.

Someone must have come to their senses, because another match was lit. It was Paul, but this time he wasn't holding it in his helmet. In front of him stood the old man extending the knife out to him, handle first.

Paul took the knife, handing it to Cole as the old man walked past Paul and out of the Bunker.

All heads now turned back to the bed as another match was lit before the one burning went out and I commented, "Man, Joe looks totally out of it."

The sight was sickening. Joe was covered with blood, his eyes wide open, but he just seemed to be staring off into empty space. His mouth was moving, but no words were coming out, and I knew he was in deep shock.

It didn't look to me like any of the others knew what to do, nor was anyone going to take charge. I really didn't know what to do either, but someone had to take charge. So I laid my rifle on the top bunk with my other things saying, "Paul, you and Cole clean Joe up, John help me with the girl."

They placed their weapons in the window as I took the girl's arms pulling them from around Joe's neck. I then took hold of her wrists as John handed Cole the matches before grasping the girl's ankles.

We carried her out of the Bunker as Cole lit his lighter.

Down next to the river, we swung her body back and forth until I said softly, "Now!" Then we let go and her body hit the water with a loud splash. We walked back to the Bunker, having paid no attention as to whether or not anyone had heard the splash.

Back in the Bunker, Cole and Paul had Joe pretty well cleaned up and we helped by cleaning up the bunk itself.

The lighter and matches were no longer lit and we did most of our work in the dark as well as calming ourselves down from the incident.

After a time, I suggested, "Okay. We don't have to say exactly what happened."

As I took a breath, trying to think of what else to say that would make sense, John spoke up, asking, "What about Joe? He doesn't look like he's going to come back anytime soon."

I lit my lighter now holding it in front of Joe's face and he lay quiet. His mouth was no longer moving, but he was still staring blankly straight ahead, seeing nothing.

I pulled my lighter away telling everyone, "Just let him lay here and hopefully he'll be fine by morning. For now, let's get to watching the river. "

Paul and Cole volunteered quickly grabbing their gear and vanished outside. John and I stood at the window, deep in our own thoughts.

From time to time, I'd go to Joe, light my lighter to see how he was doing, but he remained the same.

After a few hours, I found him with his eyes finally closed and he seemed to be resting calmly.

After a few hours, John and I relieved Paul and Cole, but no one slept at all that night.

Morning found Joe still unconscious and even shaking him did no good. We knew it was more serious than we'd previously thought.

Paul stated the obvious, "I think we've got a problem here. It's about time for the truck to pick us up." He'd no sooner got those words out when we heard the truck pull up and stop outside.

We went out and found Sergeant Baker standing beside the truck. He asked as we approached him, "What was all the light in the Bunker last night about?"

It seemed he was talking to me, because no one else was answering. I said, "Joe's in a bad way and we didn't know what's wrong. We hoped he would be fine by this morning, but he isn't. We did the best we could to help him, though." I stopped and hoped it was enough to satisfy him.

Sergeant Baker didn't say a word. He walked past us and entered the Bunker while we waited outside, hoping for the best.

Soon the Sergeant came out and instructed us, "Get on the truck, I'll wait here until help arrives."

We got our gear, climbed aboard the truck, which then crossed the bridge to pick up the others and soon we were on our way back. The Sergeant was still standing outside, watching us pass before going into the Bunker.

We got back to the base at 0830 hours and having the day off, I skipped breakfast. After showering, I went straight to bed and slept until noon.

Thanksgiving came and supper was the only thing that made it feel any different from any other day. We had a great, traditional turkey dinner, and afterward, I could hardly move from eating so much.

I found myself on the Guard Duty roster and pulled it with Danny Woods and Melvin Dollar. We were thankful the night went smoothly and we all took our turn sleeping.

The first of the month came and I decided to buy a TV. I went to the PX and bought the perfect twelve-inch TV. I took it back to the Hooch and found it could only pick up one channel. But it was crystal clear.

Going back to the PX, I bought a reel-to-reel tape recorder and four reels of tape, brought them all back to the Hooch and practiced with it until I understood how the recorder worked. Then I taped a letter home.

Christmas Eve came and I decided to work, figuring no one would show up, I wanted a quiet place to be for a while. I sat in my office typing a letter to Mom, but was soon interrupted when Sergeant Dickerson showed up. It was good seeing him again.

I opened the door and greeted him with, "Where have you been hiding yourself?"

After talking awhile, he inquired, "What's the chances of getting some more sandbags, still without paperwork?"

"It's great, just go get some men." I answered. He looked at me a little puzzled, which I assumed was due to my not asking any questions this time, so I added, "I don't ask anymore. I've learned a lot since our last meeting and you wouldn't be asking for any if you really didn't need them."

Sergeant Dickerson thanked me, saying he would be back shortly and was off.

While waiting, I thought about asking him for some whiskey when he got back. Then I realized it would be like selling my supplies and I wasn't ready to start doing that.

Twenty minutes later, he was back with two men and after they had two bundles each, Sergeant Dickerson thanked me again. They left and I went back to my office and my letter home.

Just before lunch, I saw the squad come in and it was going to be good seeing Don again.

Willie, who retrieved the mail daily from the Air Base, came by and I inquired, "Where you off to today?"

He told me, "Over here, mail comes even on Christmas Eve."

We talked for some time and I found out he lived not far from my home town.

Soon he asked, "Have you had any Boom Boom since you've been here?"

I replied, "Not yet. I've come close a couple times. Of course, until lately I wasn't wanting to, I guess. But after this long, those girls are starting to look mighty good."

Willie chuckled before saying, "Well, we can't have a guy from California go through a year over here not having a girl at least once."

I reminded him, "Remember, we can't go to the village anymore. I don't see how I can do anything about it."

Willie asked, smiling, "You going to be here in an hour?"

"I can be," I answered.

Willie smiled even broader, informing me, "If you do, I'll bring you a girl. A Christmas gift to a brother Californian. "

I liked the idea, but I couldn't figure out how it could be done the way the MP's check all vehicles coming in at the gate. So I asked, "How?"

"I've learned a few tricks to get things done. Leave that to me. You just be here in an hour when I come back." I agreed to be and he got in his truck and drove off.

After lunch, a baseball game was planned to get started. If Willie didn't make it back with a girl, I would join the game.

The next hour seemed like an eternity. Then I saw Willie's truck stop at the gate and the MP's looked the truck over thoroughly, even inside, before letting him in.

I knew if they had found the girl in the truck, Willie would be in real trouble. So when he went to the Post Office rather than coming to the yard, I figured he had changed his mind. I couldn't blame him. I locked up the office, feeling frustrated, and not wanting to hear any excuses.

That evening, I brought another case of whiskey to the Hooch. It had mysteriously appeared at my office several days earlier, just like the other one. We partied heartily. And this time there was no problem with Mike, nor the Vietnamese.

On Christmas morning, I decided to get my recorder from the office where I'd left it the day before. While I was there, Willie showed up asking, "Where were you yesterday? I brought you a girl and you weren't anywhere to be found. "

I explained, "I was here and saw the MP's search your truck. I saw you go to the Post Office, rather than here. I figured you had changed your mind, so I joined the ball game. If I had known you had a secret compartment, I would have stayed here. Sorry, I messed things up for you. It's my loss."

Willie thought a moment and then asked, "You working today?" "I wasn't going to, what have you got in mind?"

"If you're going to be here for lunch, I'll bring her in again for you. But you better mean it this time though and be here no matter what."

"Willie, I'll be here from now until you come and either tell me you have her with you or tell me you weren't able to." He responded, getting in his truck, "Okay then." And he left.

While waiting, I extended my letter to my mother and the morning really dragged along. I saw Willie's truck leave through the gate and half an hour later he returned. Once again his truck was searched the same as always before being allowed through the gate. But this time he came directly to my yard.

As he stopped beside my office and got out of the truck, I joined him and he asked, "Where do you want the truck parked while you enjoy yourself?"

I inquired a little puzzled, "Where do you have her, in your pocket? That's the only place they didn't check."

Willie laughed telling me, "Nah, she's in the back of the truck. Go take a Look."

Doubtful, I followed him to the back of the truck where he raised the flap. Up next to the cab laid a cot on its side. Behind it a girl's head appeared over the top, saw us and asked in broken English, "Where Number One GI?"

I told Willie, "I'll never doubt you again, buddy. Pull 'round the back of the yard where we'll be less conspicuous."

He did and I met him again at the back of the truck where he asked, "Is she pretty enough?"

She had moved to the tailgate of the truck and I got a good look at her. I assured him, "Oh yeah!"

So he told me, "Then get in there and enjoy yourself. Here's a rubber in case you don't have one of your own." And he pulled one from his pocket, handing it to me. I took it because in fact, I didn't have one.

I now crawled into the truck and told Willie, "Thank you, thank you, thank you! I owe you big time buddy. "

The girl and I moved to the cot and I up-righted it. Then I watched the girl as we took our clothes off, then laid on the cot together. I slipped the rubber on and wrapped my arms around the girl. It felt good having a woman's naked body against mine.

When I got out of the truck, I was exhausted. But I felt great as Willie exclaimed, "I know you did us proud."

I smiled, saying through heavy breathing, "You bet and thanks. I couldn't have had a better Christmas present. That's one I'll never forget, nor who brought her to me."

About then the girl raised the flap, still naked. She inquired, "Any more GI's?"

I spouted off, arrogantly, "Yeah, about two hundred and fifty, honey!"

She responded, smiling even bigger, "Are they here now? I be Number One girl to them all."

I looked at Willie, who informed me as if reading my mind,

"She's serious. She'd take on the whole company at five dollars a head."

I told Willie, "Thanks again for the gift. But please, get her out of here before she gets us both in trouble. "

He laughed and we shook hands as he replied, "Okay. See you tomorrow and Merry Christmas." I wished him the same and he drove off.

I went to the office and locked up. Then I headed for the Hooch and found everyone watching my TV. So I sat down, joining them.

The next day I got a letter from a girl back home that I had been living with just prior to joining the Army. Her letter told me that our daughter had a heart condition. This pissed me off, because she hadn't even told me about a pregnancy.

The following day, I got to my office late and found Joe and the workers waiting. So I announced, "Today we're going to straighten up the Conex's first and then..."

Joe interrupted, "I'll tell the workers. I don't work!"

I wasn't in the best of moods as I walked up to within a foot of him before speaking, "But you will! Just like the rest of us!"

He answered in what I considered a defiant manner, "I'm an interpreter, not a worker!"

Today of all days, he shouldn't have defied me! He'd no sooner finished speaking, when I quickly snatched the front of his shirt and twisting it, I raised him almost off the ground. I slammed him hard against the Conex, saying in a threatening tone, "You will work when I say so or else! So get your ass busy, before I really get mad and hurt you!"

I released him and he exclaimed bitterly, "I'll see you court-martialed for this!"

This fired my anger even more. I didn't touch him, but said, "You may later! But today I'm going to work your butt off! "

I motioned the workers to the shade before putting Joe to work in the Conex. Afterwards, I moved him to the lumber and worked him right through lunch.

That evening after supper, I was trying to relax in the Hooch when the Captain's runner came in and announced, "Weaver, report to the Captain right away."

I answered, "Okay." And he left as I headed for the CO's Office having a slight idea what he wanted.

I stood before the Captain's desk, at attention and reported, "Specialist Fourth Class Weaver, reporting as ordered, Sir."

He studied me for a second before asking, "Did you manhandle your interpreter this morning?"

I decided to just get it over with, so responded, "Yes Sir." He told me in a tone I knew meant business, "If you ever touch a worker again, I'll court-martial you! Do you read me, soldier? "

I replied, "Yes, Sir." And he dismissed me. So I left knowing that if I had my hands on Joe right then, I'd twist his little head off his shoulders. I also knew that I had to calm down before morning. So I watched TV, trying to relax and forget the whole thing.

I woke the next morning, still a little mad, but under control. I got up and went to breakfast before going to work.

The workers showed up, but not Joe, so we set to work anyway and it went smoothly, even without Joe.

I decided it was time to go on R & R (Rest and Recuperation). Being as it was the end of the year, I figured it would be the best way to start the New Year. So I put in for it and was told I would be leaving the next day. The irony of the whole thing was that I drew Guard Duty that night.

It started out a quiet night. My mind was mostly occupied with wondering who I was going to get at the last minute to take over my place while I was gone. I couldn't think of anyone that was in camp at the moment that had the ability to handle it.

At midnight, to bring in the New Year, all the Bunkers set off flares of every color, lighting the sky brilliantly.

The next day I got ready to go and was told there would be a day's delay in my departure. That was okay with me, because as Ron Shepard pointed out, this would be like having an extra day added to my R & R, where I had the day off anyway.

That night I sat on my cot drinking beer and watching TV alone. The rest of the squad was out on a mission. About 2200 hours, there was an explosion and I jumped up, grabbed my gear, headed out the door and down the hill to my reinforced Bunker in the lumber yard.

There were many more explosions before I got there, some even hitting the lumber yard. Once I was safely in my Bunker, I found two other guys already occupying it and said, "Welcome to my home gentlemen." I couldn't make out who they were, so I hoped this would allow them the chance to identify themselves.

They did and it was Bob and Duke from second squad whom I had talked to in the club earlier, when buying my beer.

Trying to ease the tension just as several more explosions went off even closer to the Bunker than before, I said, "If I'd have known you guys were coming to visit, I'd have arranged a quieter evening."

They started laughing, but were cut off short by multiple explosions that sounded in various places in the lumber yard. We got serious and watched for movement knowing my Bunker could take direct hits better than any other Bunker in the area. With most of the company gone, the Vietnamese might try to break through.

An hour later, the explosions got further apart. But it was still hours before morning, which couldn't come too soon for me.

The sky brightened with even more flares and I could see silhouettes moving around, but they were too tall to be Vietnamese.

It seemed like a long time now since the last explosion. I hoped that part of the night was over, though I could still hear gunfire, some within the compound itself.

There was another explosion that sounded far off. I knew it wasn't a rocket because it had a duller sound to it, more like a grenade. I broke the following silence with, "Here they come." We chambered rounds into our weapons and made ready, waiting!

A voice outside startled us before I recognized it as being Sergeant Baker's, "If anyone's in the Bunker, fall out! We have VC in the compound and need to find them."

We left the Bunker and with flares lighting up the area, we found Sergeant Baker behind a pile of lumber about twenty feet away. When he asked for our names, we told him quickly.

He then told us, "Move cautiously, they're well-armed." We spread out, keeping each other in sight.

I was just left of Baker and I asked as we moved slowly, "How many broke through Sergeant?"

He answered, "Three or four. No one knows for sure." We moved out slowly and carefully in somewhat of a crooked line, passing other Bunkers and picking up more men from each, leaving one man to protect the area we just covered. Our line steadily grew.

Up ahead a small figure jumped up running and before I could get a round off, several other weapons opened up and the figure fell to the ground hard and we walked on.

The line advanced slowly, keeping all eyes on another figure on the ground. We stopped about twenty meters from it and Sergeant Baker called out, "Everyone down until I see what he has."

I dropped behind a telephone pole, my rifle aimed at the figure and waited, thankful that more flares lit up the area.

It was clearly a Vietnamese man lying there, motionless on his belly, his arms tucked underneath him. Sergeant Baker moved toward the guy with another man whom appeared beside him.

The guy with Baker got ahead and bent down to roll the figure over, when Baker tackled the guy. Both vanished and I figured they had landed in a ditch. I couldn't understand why Baker had done that. Then he called from wherever he was, below ground level, "The guys alive and boobytrapped." Then Baker started talking in Vietnamese so fast, I couldn't catch enough to understand.

I finally asked the guy close by, "What's he saying?"

The guy told me, "He's telling him to get up and stop playing possum or he'll be blown away for nothing."

I just remarked, "Oh, thanks."

Now Sergeant Baker called out in English, "Who's got the 'Sixty?"

A voice answered, "All set and ready for action."

Sergeant Baker ordered, "Put a burst alongside him and don't worry if a few rounds hit his legs." Immediately rounds started kicking up sand from next to his head, down his side and the last few rounds hit his legs and feet. But the guy still didn't roll over, he just cried out in pain.

Sergeant Baker spoke in Vietnamese again. To no avail, for the man still didn't move. Baker then ordered, "Blow the bastard off whatever he's covering up."

The 'Sixty opened up on the body and I could see most of the rounds hitting their mark, riddling the Vietnamese body as it jerked and bucked, puffs of flesh and clothing exploding from the body where the rounds exited and soon the body rolled over.

Before the guy with the 'Sixty stopped firing, there was the most deafening explosion. I released my weapon laying on the ground, covered my ears and helmet and closed my eyes, I could hear fragments whistling past and hoped I wouldn't get hit.

When the dust settled, I looked around, my ears ringing and saw several figures rising up. I got up and followed them to what was left of the body. When I got a look, I almost threw up but held it down as I walked on. I saw several men gathered around the spot in which Baker and the other guy had vanished.

As I approached, I heard someone ask, "Are they dead?"

I saw a guy I didn't know kneel down beside Baker and the other guy which I now recognized as Eddy. The guy kneeling down announced, "They're both in bad shape, Danny go for help."

I inquired, "Is there anything we can do to help?"

He answered, "No. But there are still VC out there needing to be found. But carefully, don't make more work like this for me."

Realizing he was a medic, we spread out as it grew dark again.

We continued on as more flares now lit the area back up.

Off in the distance, gunfire erupted and our line squatted, waiting to see what developed. But we remained ready and alert.

When the shooting died out, word came down that three more Vietnamese had been found and killed. That was all there was. It was clear now, so I went back to the Hooch and found my TV still on, but the station was off. I sat in the dark, on my cot, watching the snow on the screen while I shook violently all over, unable to control myself.

Phil came in and sat down without a word.

After a while, I asked, "How's Baker and Eddy?"

He informed me, "They'll be just fine after a few days' rest. They looked worse than they really were. They survived only because they were below ground level, suffering just concussions."

Daylight came and Fred stuck his head in the door announcing, "They got a dead gook out at the inner perimeter, Bunker Five, I was told you would be interested in seeing, Ward. You've been told, so go check it out."

After he left, I commented, "I wonder what that's all about?"

Phil answered, "I don't know, but let's go find out." I shrugged and we headed for inner Bunker Five.

We found a bunch of guys standing around a body on the ground. Tim saw me and called out, "Hey Weaver. This should really cheer you up."

I didn't answer, but wondered how a dead body could cheer me up. I found out when I stopped at the body and saw who it was. I smiled big. Tim had been right.

There, before me, laid Joe, the Vietnamese that had almost gotten me court-martialled. I asked, "Anyone got a camera? I need a picture of this." He looked a mess and I asked, "How many times was he hit?"

Joe's body laid in an unnatural manner, face down in the sand. Tim told me, "I'll get my thirty-five millimeter camera. He was hit thirty-six times before hitting the ground. Anthony never misses. He emptied two clips in him."

Tim pointed at the pit in the sand, halfway between us and the Bunker and continued, "There's where the satchel charge landed that he was intending to throw into the Bunker."

I just replied, "WOW!" Tim left to get his camera.

A satchel charge is a sandbag filled with explosives, tied off with a blasting cap inside and a detonator attached. When ready, the pin is pulled on the detonator and the bag is tossed to wherever it's intended. It goes off, killing everyone in its immediate area, in this case, the inside of a Bunker.

Tim was soon back and started taking pictures of Joe as I inquired, "How are you going to get that film developed? We're not exactly supposed to have these kinds of pictures."

Tim assured me, "Don't worry, I have a guy over at the Main Post that does all my developing."

I admitted, "Sounds great and I appreciate this."

Tim told me, "After what he did last night and almost did to you, it's my pleasure. You'll have them in a couple days." I thanked him and left.

Approaching the Hooch, I saw people moving here and there. The company was getting back to some kind of order.

Back in the Hooch, I got ready for breakfast. I wasn't scheduled to leave until 1500 hours and sleep was out of the question!

After breakfast, I decided to go to the office and wait in the coolness of my fan. Once there, I sat and watched my relief and the workers fill sandbags.

A knock on the door startled me. I saw it was Lieutenant Lee, so I let him in, asking, "What can I do for you today, Sir?" He replied, "I need some sandbags, Ward. Could you help me again? For as usual, l don't have any paperwork."

I was happy to. I exclaimed, "Sure, bring some men over and I'll take care of you. But hurry, for I'm going on R & R in a few hours."

"Thanks," he replied, rushing out and headed down the road. Ten minutes later he was back with three men, Lieutenant Lee told his men to place their weapons in the corner of my office, which they did along with his. Then we went to the Conex where I opened the door saying, "Get what you need."

All four picked up two bundles apiece, shouldering them. I locked the door and we headed back to my office.

Arriving, Lieutenant Lee said, "Thank you again for these, Ward, and have a good time on your R & R."

"You're welcome and I'm sure I will," I replied as they walked on.

I watched them for a long time before going back into my office, where just inside the door, I spotted the weapons and rushing back outside, I yelled, "Hey, Lieutenant Lee!" He and his men stopped and looked back as I reported, "You forgot your weapons."

He called back, "No, we didn't. Those are yours as souvenirs for all the help you've given us. See you later."

"But you're going to need them," I said after him.

He answered, "We'll get more, don't worry. Just enjoy and thank you." Then they turned and continued on their way. So I went back into my office and looked my new gifts over.

One was a bolt action AK-44 which I recognized as used by snipers. Another was an automatic AK-47; the third was what I had heard referred to as a Tommy gun, but I'd never seen one in real life until now. The fourth was so unusual that I'd never even seen a picture of that one.

I put them back in the corner, sat down and tried to figure out what to do with them while I was on R & R. I couldn't mail them home, yet if I was caught with them, I'd be in trouble.

Finally, I took them to my private Conex, placed them under a layer of sandbags, padlocked the door, and hoped they would be safe until I got back. Then I could think of what to do with them.

After lunch, Ron found me in the Hooch and asked, "Is there anything in particular you want done while you're gone?"

I answered, "Nah, just keep track of everything that comes in and goes out. I'll enter them in my books when I get back. "Sounds easy enough," Ron responded.

Then I added, "There is one thing. The far Conex from the office is where I keep personal gear. I keep it locked and there's no reason why you need to get in there. I'll hold you responsible for what's in there until I get back."

Ron exclaimed, "I'm here to give out and take in materials until you get back. So you can count on those doors staying closed until then. Okay?"

We shook hands, then just sat around talking about home and I found out he was from Virginia.

Before leaving, I told him I'd left the fan for him to use. He said he appreciated it and then I caught a jeep to the airport.

I got on board a C-130 cargo plane, which took me to Da Nang where I had an overnight layover.

I took this time to see my ex-brother-in-law. My youngest sister's ex-husband, whom I still considered a brother-in-law.

I had a letter from Barry with his return address on it. So I hailed a cab, showed the driver the address and was taken to a building on the Marine Base. Inside it I found Barry and he introduced me to his fellow workers and bosses.

Because I was still two ranks below him, I couldn't go to the Officers' Club, as he wanted to do after work. So he took me to his Hooch and laid out one of his uniforms telling me to put it on and meet him back at the office and he left.

Barry and I were about the same build, so my being a few inches taller made no difference. The uniform fit perfectly.

On my way back to the office, I was saluted by privates. I returned their salute just to be safe and asked Barry about that upon arriving.

He laughed a little before explaining that in the Marines,

Sergeants and above get saluted. I was only used to Lieutenants and above getting saluted in the Army.

After Barry got off work, we went to the Officers Club where we drank until the place closed. Then we staggered to his Hooch and called it a night.

The next morning, I dressed in my own uniform, said goodbye to Barry and got a cab to the airport.

Once there, I boarded a Boeing 707 to Bangkok, Thailand.

After landing, we were instructed on their traditional customs: Not to make body contact in public with the girls we would be having. How to exchange our money to theirs (which was called a Baht, with an exchange rate of seven Baht to one American dollar) and finally we were taken by bus to a fine hotel.

Inside, I asked the clerk for a room for five days and was told that would cost a Hundred and Twenty-five Baht.

I held out my money asking the clerk to help me and as he took some bills from my hand, I hoped he wasn't cheating me. Then I signed the card he placed before me and a bellboy took my bag. He led me to my room on the third floor.

After he placed my bag on the bed, I handed him a bill which seemed to offend him. Figuring I'd underpaid him, I gave him another which seemed to please him very much. Now I was sure he'd been overpaid. But I was there to enjoy myself, not worry about money.

* * *

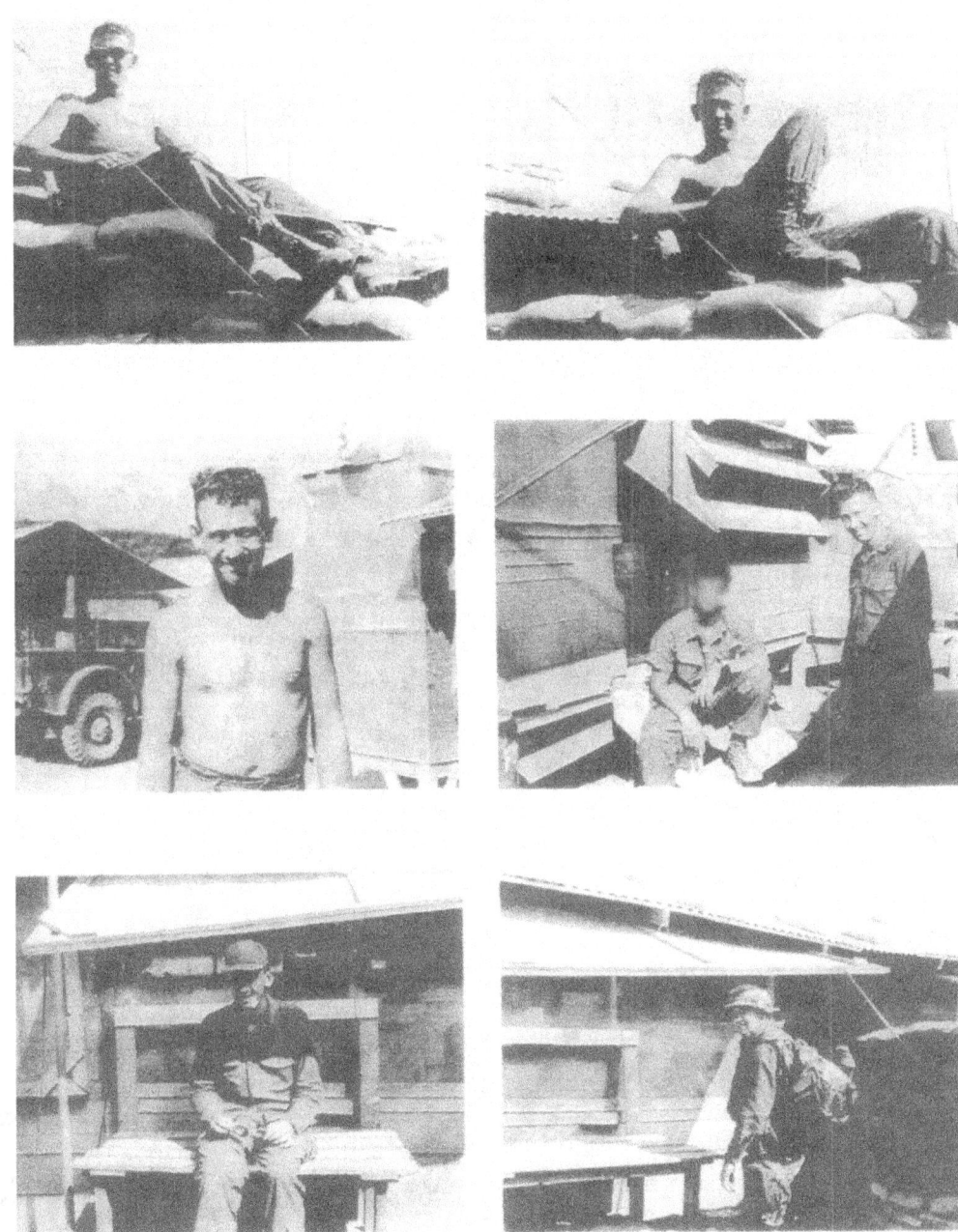

* * *

I showered and changed into civilian clothes. Then I went down to the desk and questioned the clerk. I held out the same kind of bill I had given the bellboy the second time and asked, "How much is this in American money?"

The clerk told me, "Twenty American dollars, sir."

I thanked him, put the money away, and inquired further, "How's the best way to get around here?"

He informed me, "Most GIs buy a cab and driver for their stay. That way, anytime you want to go someplace, just pick up the phone in your room and the cab will be waiting when you come down. They are also your interpreters, unless you speak our language."

It sounded good, so I asked, "How much?" And was told a Hundred and Twenty-five Baht for the whole week.

I paid and a man was called over. The clerk talked to him in their language for a while before he was introduced to me, "This is Al, your driver."

I shook Al's hand and he asked in good English, "Where do you want to go first?"

Not knowing, I inquired, "Where do most GI's start?"

Al thought a moment before answering, "I guess a massage parlor and I know Number One place. We go now?"

"Okay," I said and followed him out of the hotel. Since I'd never had a steam bath and massage, so I thought this would start off my R & R in the best way I could hope for.

In the cab, we raced through the streets and I leaned forward at one point to see the speedometer. We were doing a hundred kilometers per hour, so I asked, "Aren't you going a tad fast? What if a pedestrian steps out in front of you?"

Al just replied, "They shouldn't have and they know better." Curious, I inquired, "You mean cars have the right of way over people walking?"

"That's right." So I sat back pondering this.

We stopped in front of a long building and we got out. I followed Al inside where immediately, a young boy appeared. He handed us a glass each, with a dark liquid and ice in it.

I took a sip and found out it was Coco-Cola. It was very cold and felt good going down my throat.

A very large woman with a nice smile came in. "Can I help you?" she asked, and I was surprised at how good her English was.

"I'd like a steam bath and massage please," I said.

She replied, "That will be twenty-five Baht, sir."

With Al's help, I paid. Then Al sat on a bench by the door and I followed the lady across the room to a curtain that hung from the ceiling to the floor. It covered the whole wall, from one side to the other side of the room, completely hiding whatever was behind it.

She pushed a button on the adjacent wall and the curtain slid open, revealing a one-way mirror the same height and width as the curtain. On the other side of the mirror was a room containing about a hundred girls of every size, shape, and form. They were all wearing white mini-dress uniforms.

Above their left breast was a red tag with a white number on it. I was so engrossed, I almost didn't hear the woman ask, "Which girl would you like?"

My eyes drifted over the sea of beautiful girls before I picked number fifty-five. The boy who had given us the coke upon arriving left to retrieve the girl.

As the girl entered the room, the woman informed me, "This is Kim, and she will take care of you." And with that, Kim took my hand, then led me down a hall and into a room.

It was a small room containing a big square metal box with a hole in the top, a bathtub and a table on wheels.

The girl said something, but I couldn't understand. When I didn't react, she reached over and unbuttoned my shirt. I let her do that, but when she started to undo my pants, I took over and soon I stood in just my shorts.

She handed me a towel, which I put around my waist and at her instructions, pulled my shorts off as well.

Now the girl slipped out of her dress and stood in just her panties and bra. She opened the front of the metal box before motioning for me to get in. I did and sat on the stool inside it. Then she closed the door with my head sticking up through the hole in the top. She turned a dial on the side of the box before leaving the room.

It got very hot inside the box and with my long legs, my knees kept touching the metal wall and I kept getting burned no matter how hard I tried to keep them from touching the wall.

Sweat ran down my face and got in my eyes burning and my vision was now blurred. I had no way of wiping my eyes, trapped like I was, until the girl returned to let me out.

Soon a bell went off and I thought that at last I was going to get out. I thought that it had to be the timer. But time passed and she didn't return.

When the bell went off two more times about five minutes apart, she finally rushed in and turned the machine off, letting me out and started speaking fast. I figured she was apologizing and I let it pass, thankful to be out of that box.

Kim motioned for me to get on the table, so I did with my face down. I watched her body as she walked to the side of the table and turned it lengthwise, against the bathtub half filled with water. Then she quickly jerked her side of the table up, causing me to roll sideways, off the table and into the tub containing ice water that I swore came directly out of the North Pole.

I jumped out of the water swearing and stood shivering, doing my best to keep from yelling further as the girl rushed out of the room.

Alone I gathered my clothes remembering hearing what she did was how pores in the skin are quickly closed.

I finished dressing realizing I was not going to get a massage. I found my way back to where I had started and told Al, "Man that was pure hell."

He replied, "You look better." And I knew he was lying.

The woman, I realized now, was the Madam of the place, came in and asked, "You want to buy a girl?"

I responded boldly, "I've never paid for a lay... except for maybe once, but I was so drunk, I don't..."

Al interrupted, taking my arm, "For twenty-five Baht, she will be yours from now until morning. It is the way here."

I thought about this a moment before inquiring, "Will she go everywhere with me?"

Al replied, "Yes, she'll go and do whatever she can to please you; however, she can."

So I told the Madam, "Yes. I'd like a girl. Do you pick her or have one in mind?"

Smiling, she said, pushing the button again, causing the curtain to open like it had before, "Same as with the steam bath girl."

As I looked through the glass, I was thinking of having paid for a massage I didn't get. Suddenly seeing the vision through the glass, I didn't care and was like a kid in a candy store, but only being allowed one piece.

Though these were the same girls, what made it different from the first time around was that at that time I thought they were only for the steam bath and massages. But now I could pick one as a companion until morning.

Sitting in the far corner of the room was a very young girl whose number was #2, which seemed appropriate somehow. I told the woman the number and the girl was brought out. I asked her, "Do you speak English?" She shook her head.

'Oh well,' I thought. I had Al to interpret for us and sex didn't need any translation. I paid for three days with her, not knowing if I wanted a woman on my birthday in four days.

We rode to the hotel in silence. I was staring at her all the way. She was gorgeous and her smile was enchanting in a mystical way.

At the hotel, I asked Al to get her name for me. After talking to her in their language for a moment, he finally told me.

"Her name is Pam and she just turned eighteen, if you're interested?"

I was and then told him, "Thank you. I'll call down when we are ready to go somewhere." He nodded as Pam and I headed for the elevator and my room.

Once inside, I took her into my arms, hers went around me and we kissed. Her lips were wonderful, just as was her petite body molding against mine.

When I released her, she went to the bed and began to undress. She was even more ravishing without clothes.

She then started removing my clothes and I let her. Soon we both stood before each other, naked as the day we were born. She then led me into the bathroom where we showered together.

Later on, we showered again and then we got dressed to go out and I picked up the phone telling the voice that answered, "This is Weaver in room 303. I'll need my cab in about five minutes."

He replied, "Yes, sir. He will be ready." And I hung up.

Pam had put on an even shorter mini dress than her uniform had been, but this one was white with many different colorful flower prints on it. Then we left finding Al in the lobby.

As we approached him, he asked, "Where to first?"

I looked at Pam and then told Al, "I'm in her hands."

Al and Pam talked in their language for a while before he told me, "She wonders if you would like to see our Temples?"

I responded, "Yes, that sounds great." So we were off.

Our first stop was a very large and beautiful Temple. Pam and I headed inside while Al stayed in the cab.

The building had, sloping oriental roofs like I had only seen in pictures. Inside, Pam stepped out of her shoes. Then she pointed at mine and I realized that she wanted me to remove mine as well, so I did. Then she led me through the place which was colorful and beautiful.

After a couple of hours and back in the cab, I told Al,

"Tell Pam I thought the place was beautiful and appreciated her showing it to me."

He spoke to her a few moments and she smiled at me, which I took as pleasing her. Then we were off to our next stop.

It turned out to be a parking lot at the base of a high mountain peak. As we got out, I inquired, "What's here?"

Al explained, "She wants to show you the oldest Temple in Bangkok." And he pointed at the steps tracing up the mountain.

"Wonder how many steps are there?" I asked, not really expecting an answer.

But Al told me, "Three thousand and sixty steps."

I could see a hole in the side of the mountain almost at the top and curiosity made me say, "Let's get going."

Almost to the top, I had to take a break, but once inside, it was worth the climb. Besides being beautiful, inside there were gorgeous statues of various types in crevices in the walls throughout the place.

We stayed for about an hour and the trip down was much easier. Back at the cab, Al asked me, "Have you ever seen a five-legged bull before?" I had been raised on a farm, but had never seen one. So I told him I hadn't and he remarked, "Come with me and I'll show you one." Pam accompanied us and under the shade of a tree stood a very large Brahman bull, muzzled and staked to the ground with a long rope.

Sure enough, hanging from its left hip was a fully developed leg and hoof. I could tell it was useless to the animal and wondered if maybe someone had grafted it on to attract tourists. So I asked, "Can we pet it?" Al nodded, leading us to the animal.

It didn't stop eating. So moving to its hindquarters, I parted the short hair looking for a scar. I couldn't find one and I finally realized this animal had in fact been born a freak of nature.

After that, we left and looking at my watch, we had missed lunch by quite a bit. We weren't really hungry, so we went back to the hotel, where Pam and I made love before showering and dressing for the evening.

Pam now wore a matching white mini-skirt and blouse.

We met Al in the lobby and I asked him to inquire if she liked dancing. After a brief conversation between them, he told me she did. So our first stop was a nice restaurant, where I let her order to try one of their traditional foods.

Then we went to a place where they had a live band so we could dance.

The place was packed and the only seats seeming available were two stools at the bar. We took them and ordered a couple of drinks.

As I took a sip, an elbow hit me, spilling my drink and almost knocking me off the stool. Figuring it was an accident, I was willing to let it pass. I got another drink and ignored the incident. But as I took another sip, the elbow hit me harder than before. I came off the stool, madder than hell and wanted to find out who had done it.

Standing a few feet away from me smiling menacingly was a really big white guy, looking like he wanted trouble. And I was more than willing to accommodate him.

I started for the guy when a hand grabbed my shirt sleeve. I looked back to see who wanted a piece of me first, but it was only Pam. She spoke in barely a whisper, but surprisingly audible English, "I take care."

I almost laughed, her suggestion was so funny. I wasn't sure I could take this giant ape of a man. But here was this mere slip of a girl, not even five foot tall and weighing maybe eighty pounds. She was going to take him on? I'd heard of David and Goliath, but this match-up would put them to shame.

I shook my head saying as slowly as possible, hoping she would understand, "No girl fights my battles." And I turned to pursue my destiny as she let go of my shirt.

A hand grabbed my other sleeve. I turned to find it was the bartender leaning over the bar. He spoke to me in good English, "I don't want to tell you what to do Mister, but if you don't let her handle it, you disrespect her as your woman. She's been trained to protect her man since she was a little girl."

I asked arrogantly, but joking, "How about the men?"

He replied seriously, "We learn on our own."

I exclaimed, "Okay. She's one of yours. If you want her killed, who am I to stand in the way?" So I sat back on the stool as Pam got off hers, now smiling at me.

Pam boldly walked up to the guy, saying in her best English, "You apologize my man."

The big gorilla laughed, crossing his arms and responded, "Go sit down little girl before you get hurt." He quickly reached out to push her, but she avoided it. That made the guy apparently angrier, for he stepped forward, taking a swing at Pam and swearing, "Damn bitch!"

Pam quickly avoided the swing, raised her mini-skirt, tucking it inside the top of her panties, not caring who saw. Pam seemed to literally walk up the front of the guy's body to his face. The heel of her right foot seemed to drive into his nose, catapulting her backward and landing like a cat on her feet.

I sat in awe as the big ape toppled over backward like a felled Oak tree. Pam readjusted her skirt and crawled back onto the stool, took my hand and smiled at me.

I held onto her hand with one of mine, keeping my eyes locked on hers as I picked up my drink and took a swallow, still in disbelief.

I ordered another drink, needing it and as I paid for it, the bartender gave me a wink that broke the ice that had formed inside me and I nodded back to him. I looked back at Pam, smiling. She sat her drink down and leaving mine on the counter, I lifted her off the stool. Then holding her hand, we went to the dance floor.

Our first dance was a slow one and we held each other close as we moved to the music. She was a fantastic dancer.

I never took my eyes off Pam the whole evening. The band played the same kind of Rock-N-Roll music as back home in the States, we danced more often than we sat them out.

We finally got a table, but we spent very little time at it. Time didn't seem to exist now. Only her smile and laughter existed to me, along with my holding her during the slow dances.

With the Thailand beer being eighteen percent alcohol, it wasn't long before I was feeling overly happy.

During a fast dance, I took the sombrero from a musician who didn't object, I put it on as Pam and I continued dancing. This caused Pam to laugh at how I looked. Her laugh was so contagious, I started laughing as well.

During the next fast dance, I left Pam at the foot of the stage and climbing upon it, I stood next to the guy I took the sombrero from him and he smiled big. Then he handed me the maracas he was playing and nodded. I had never played an instrument, but being drunk now, I didn't care. I shook them to the music and the band played on.

Everyone seemed to be having a great time. Even Pam was standing there, cheering me on, clapping. It was a perfect night.

When the song was over, I gave the musician back his maracas and Sombrero, thanked him and he bowed to me. I left the stage and rejoined Pam and we danced on, laughing and enjoying ourselves.

I awoke, wondering where I was and afraid to open my eyes to find out. My head felt bigger than whatever room I was in.

I finally opened my eyes and found myself in my own bed, back at the hotel. I turned over and found Pam lying beside me, sound asleep. I was glad to see her there because I wanted her again.

After showering, we dressed and met Al in the lobby, where Pam and Al talked for a moment before Al informed me, "She wants to know if you enjoy boat rides?"

I replied, "I love boats and fishing. Actually, anything dealing with the water. Why?"

Al told me, "She wants to take you boat riding and fishing."

"Great," I said, and we were off.

Soon coming to what looked like a wide canal. We got into a long narrow boat with a man in the back, who operated the outboard motor. It wasn't long before we were off.

On both sides of the canal, there were buildings weathered with time. Some having nets on poles hanging out over the water, ready to drop into the water to trap any fish going by. I was finally seeing these people as they really lived and I took in everything.

Soon the boat docked and after helping Pam out of the boat, we walked to a small building. I rented the fishing poles and bought some bait and we started fishing in an oblong pond.

I wondered what kind of fish we were fishing after and got my answer seconds after throwing my line in. I pulled out a catfish about six inches long. Then we caught several more fish and gave them to a little boy who was fishing beside us and not doing very well. His mother, sitting on the other side of him from me, really appreciated our giving them our catch.

Before leaving, we ate hot dogs and washed them down with coke.

I helped Pam back into the boat and we returned to Al and the cab, then headed back to the hotel.

Later, Al asked me if I would like to see Thailand boxing. I was delighted with the idea, so we were taken to one.

Thailand boxing was different from anything I'd ever witnessed before. Al explained that it was really kick-boxing where each bout lasted three minutes and there were three rounds to each match.

They wore much larger gloves than any I had ever seen before and they were allowed to use their elbows, feet, knees, and head in combat. I found the whole thing very interesting.

It was late when we left and the night lights of the city were inviting, but I wanted to spend the rest of the evening alone with Pam.

We ate in the hotel's beautiful dining room. We ate in silence while I watched her, knowing that the evening and the rest of the night we'd have was going to be perfect.

The next day we took in a movie. However, while I couldn't understand a word of it, I lucked out because the subtitles were in English.

Afterward, we went shopping. The first stop was a man's clothing store where Al stayed in the cab after telling me, "You pick out what you want and Pam will talk for you. They like to argue over price, but Pam will get you a fair price."

Inside a young boy came up handing us a glass of cola with ice. As hot as it was outside, it felt good going down.

After buying myself a suit, I put it on and wore it out. Our next stop was a nice little restaurant that Pam picked out and she ordered once again for me in hopes I would like maybe a different dish.

The food was still too spicy for my likes, but at least this time I enjoyed it anyway.

For the afternoon, she took me to a beautiful garden where we spent hours looking at everything in full bloom. Pam being there just enhanced the beauty of the place.

Later, she took us to a small petting zoo. She was like a child with the animals and I would have loved to have had a camera right then. No one else around us had one either, so I contented myself with just watching her.

The next morning I awoke feeling sorry for myself. It was my twenty-fourth birthday. I decided all I wanted to do was to be alone, feel sorry for myself and get drunk. So I had Al take Pam home after breakfast.

When he got back, I told him of my wish to get drunk for my birthday and he informed me, "When a GI shows it's his birthday at a bar, he only pays for the first three beers, after that they're free for the rest of the night."

I spent most of the day just laying around in my room, feeling more and more sorry for myself. I had no idea as to why or what it stemmed from.

I ate lunch in the hotel snack bar and at 1800 hours I met Al in the lobby. We were headed for a bar he said would suit me.

While we drove, Al told me about the difference between parlor girls and bar girls. Even though I had explained that I didn't want a girl at all tonight, I still listened.

"When a girl is ready to leave home, it is an honorable profession for her to work in a massage parlor as a prostitute. There, they are checked out by a doctor after every guy they have sex with. Every girl carries a medical card and if she catches a disease, no matter how slight, she can never get her medical card stamped again by a doctor. This means she can never work out of a massage parlor again. These are the girls who can be found in the bars and they may carry diseases. But they can be gotten for six to ten Baht for the night. One has to be careful."

I smiled, understanding now how the place got its nickname

that I had heard so often: "CLAP City." I told Al, "Don't worry, tonight I'm just getting drunk."

The place inside was pleasant enough with a live band and we were seated next to a rope around the dance floor. After showing the waitress proof that it was my birthday, I ordered and paid for three beers. She placed a card on the table and I assumed it indicated that my beers from then on would be free and I started drinking.

Beer, other than on tap, came in quart bottles and were the smallest drinks there and it wasn't long before I was feeling the effects.

Even my depression started vanishing, as the live band played on and I watched couples dancing.

Two young girls dancing together kept catching my eye and I figured they were waiting for some guy to ask them to dance.

One of the girls saw me watching them and started motioning with her index finger for me to come out and join her dancing.

I looked at Al who informed me, "It costs to dance here. That's why the rope is here." And he took hold of it.

I replied, "I've never paid to dance in my life and I'm not about to start now."

So Al told me, "Then you can't dance." I shook my head taking another drink, heavily depressed again.

We sat there drinking and I'd look at the girls, who continued taunting me to come dance with her. But then I would look at Al, who would shake his head, and my frustration built even more.

I was now well into my free beers when finally the girl got to me and one more indication to come out did it. When I looked at Al, he again shook his head. I raised my right hand, extended only my middle finger, then I got up, stepped over the rope and headed for the girl on the dance floor. I was drunk enough that if anyone had tried to stop me, we were going to fight. This was my birthday and I was going to dance and for free.

The girl enticing me sent her friend away and she held out her hands to me. I took them and we started dancing to the fast American Rock-N-Roll music.

After several more dances, I went to the table, keeping the girl with me. Never stepping over the rope, I drank more beer to cool off. I even let her drink from my bottle to quench her thirst before we headed back out to the dance floor.

Several dances later, the band started playing one of my favorite pieces to dance to, called "RING OF FIRE." The floor got so crowded, I kept bumping into people, even though I tried not to. But I wasn't letting it stop me from dancing with this girl. It was as if we were meant to dance together, because we were great together.

Soon I couldn't understand why I was no longer bumping into people as the music seemed to go on and on. I took a quick glance around me and was astonished beyond my wildest dreams. The people must have thought the girl and I were good as well. They had made a circle around us, clapping to the music and encouraging us on. The girl and I smiled at each other, nodding in unison and then let ourselves go as the same song went on and on and on...

I opened my eyes, wondering where I was. When had I left the bar and when did the dance end? The last thing I remembered was that girl and me dancing to those people encircling us. I wasn't even sure it was my bed I was in, but

I hoped it was as I wished my head belonged to someone else.

I slowly raised the covers, confirming my feeling of being completely naked. That created even more questions, because I never slept nude unless...

I suddenly had the feeling that I was not alone in bed. I slowly rolled over and there, lying beside me, was the girl I had been dancing with the night before. She looked even more like a child than she had the night before. I raised the covers off her, hoping to find her still clothed. Fear quickly engulfed me, seeing she was as naked as I was.

I jumped out of bed, wondering what to do next, saying to myself loudly, "You really did it this time Ward. Here you are in a foreign country in bed with a minor, a child."

I knew any second the police would burst into the room hanging me by my Jewels, never giving me a chance. Damn, how I wished to be back in Vietnam right now.

I shook her, asking as her eyes opened, "How old are you?"

She shrugged and I realized we had a language problem. I asked a different question making a square with my fingers, "Card, card. Where's your card?"

She now seemed to understand. She took her purse off the nightstand, took a card out and handed it to me, then she laid back down and continued to watch me.

I couldn't make out her name, but I was able to see clearly that she had just turned thirteen and the age rang in my head like thunder.

I sat down. My legs would no longer support me. Who would believe I hadn't done anything? Hell, I didn't believe it and I couldn't remember doing anything.

I picked up the phone and told the voice that answered, "This is Weaver in 303. Send my driver up to my room right away."

The voice answered, "Yes, sir." And I hung up.

I quickly dressed and then handed the girl her clothes saying, "Please, dress." She must have understood for she did.

I jumped at the knock on the door and then called out, "Who is it?"

Fearing it was the Bangkok Police, I almost collapsed when Al's voice announced, "You wanted to see me?"

I gave a sigh of relief and quickly opened the door. After shutting it behind him, I pointed at the girl asking, "Where did she come from and how did we get here?" I hoped he had the answer for I really needed to know.

Al explained, smiling big, "You bought her last night and had a good time. You were very happy all night, lots of fun. Here's a picture of you with the girl, leaving." And he handed me a picture from his pocket.

It was me all right, leaning against the cab, my arm over the girl's shoulders. That girl now stood in front of the mirror, brushing her hair. I did appear to have had a great time, though I couldn't remember a thing beyond that special dance.

I laid the picture on the nightstand, then told Al as I reached for my wallet, "I'll give her some money and you..."

Al interrupted, "She has been paid. She will just leave and it will all be okay."

I said, leaving my wallet in my pocket, "Take her someplace. I don't want her leaving here alone. Please Al." He nodded, took her hand, and headed for the door.

I didn't relax completely until Al was back inquiring, "What do you want to do for the rest of the day here?"

I counted my money before asking, "What do you recommend for fifty-two Baht and some change?"

He told me simply, "Get a girl and spend the night here." I told him, "I'm in your hands until the money runs out." The parlor he took me to was like the other one, but in another area. The procedure, however, was the same, except this madam was thin.

I looked over the girls behind the glass and they were all very beautiful. But I noticed one standing off by herself. The others seeming to be avoiding her. So I requested her number, which was ninety-one.

When she was brought out, I asked, "Do you speak English?" She answered in very good English, "Yes, I do."

"Great." I replied, adding, "Do you like to dance?" She shook her head and I inquired further, "How about drinking?"

She exclaimed, "You look like nice American and deserve someone who likes the same things and show you a good time. I go get right girl for you."

She turned to walk away, but I reached out taking hold of her arm gently, stopped her and said, "I want you." And I had no doubt whatsoever about my decision being the right one.

I knew these girls would do just about anything for money, but here was a girl who thought more of my feelings than money. So I was sure this girl would go out of her way to show me a good time and it wouldn't cost me beyond what I had. I paid for her and we left.

The girl said as we rode back to the hotel, "My name is Sue. What is yours?"

I told her, "Ward. So tell me about yourself."

"Well." she started, "I have been working for Kem Chu almost a year now. I am twenty-three and have a little girl..."

I broke in, "You're married with a children?"

Sue looked hurt now saying, "I am not married. I am a respectable girl and have an honorable job with Kem Chu. My child's father was killed just after we married and..."

I interrupted quickly, "I'm sorry for opening my big mouth. Let's start over. I have a big mouth sometimes." I extended my hand to her, as if to shake hands and continued, "Hi. My name is Ward. Sometimes, I'm an idiot. What's your name?"

She smiled and then giggled, surprising me by taking my hand, and saying, "I accept your apology." And we talked about different things all the way back to the hotel.

Back in my room, I asked, "Have you eaten yet?"

"I had a big breakfast. Have you eaten? "

"No. Big hangover from last night. I couldn't eat right now anyway. I just wondered if you had. So what would like to do first?" I fell silent, waiting for her answer.

Sue took my hand and answered, "Well, I have told you about me. How about we sit and you tell me about you? Please?"

I told her about myself as we sat on the bed and she seemed interested in everything I said. Eventually, I finished with a question, "And that about covers me. Were you born here in Bangkok? "

She nodded answering, "I have lived here all my life."

I knew it was past lunch now as I asked, "You hungry yet, even a little?"

"Maybe a little. What kind of food you like?"

"I'm in your hands, you lead, I follow; you feed, I eat." She laughed loudly and I enjoyed her laugh.

We met Al in the lobby and with Sue directing, our first stop was a pizza parlor where Sue asked, "I hope this is okay? I just love pizza."

I announced, "I love pizza as well." We ordered one with everything and soft drinks to wash it down with.

Our next stop was a museum where we spent several hours looking over artifacts of Thailand's past, my interest running with their weapons and farming tools.

Outside, I told Sue how great I thought it was and that there was so much history in her country and she seemed pleased I was enjoying myself. Then she informed me that there was one special place to her that she wanted to show me before we went back. So I told her, "Lead on."

She directed and soon we parked in front of a tower and I asked, "What's here?"

Smiling, she answered devilishly, "Wait and see."

We entered the tower, which was higher than any building I had seen since leaving the States. We got on an elevator and it took us to the top. I found us on an observation platform that encircled the tower.

People were everywhere. Children were playing as Sue and I looked over the view from up there. It was all breathtaking. I could see out beyond what I imagined to be the city limits as I commented, "It looks like we're seeing all of Bangkok from up here." She confirmed that and I put several coins into the telescope for Sue and me to get a clear look at different spots she wanted to point out to me.

When we left, I asked, "Where to next hon..." I caught myself from finishing that last word not wanting to offend her.

Still smiling, she announced, "I'm hungry for spaghetti. Does that sound good to you?"

I couldn't believe this girl and I had so many things in common, as I declared, "Sure does. Is there a place that makes good sauce? That is what counts with spaghetti."

"The best. Just wait and see."

We arrived about fifteen minutes later and the food was every bit as good as she claimed. We ate until we couldn't force any more food down.

Back in the lobby of the hotel, I shook Al's hand thanking him for all his help. He said it was his pleasure and left.

Sue and I went up to my room. We showered and then I counted my money. I had six Baht and some change left.

With a towel wrapped around me, I answered a knock at the door. It was the bellboy who remarked, "The manager warmly invites you and your friend to a party in honor of all the GI's at the hotel before having to leave in the morning. All the food and drinks are free." I said we would attend and he replied, "Very well, sir." Then he headed for the next door.

I closed the door, turned to find Sue standing behind me with a towel wrapped around her. I explained about the party and added, "I know you don't like parties, but ..."

She interrupted me, "We go anyway." And she dropped the towel.

I was awestruck, looking down at her naked body. Finally I spoke, "We won't stay long..." I exhaled loudly and then took a deep breath before continuing, "I assure you, we won't be staying long... no, not long at all."

She giggled and then we came into each other's arms, kissing. Then we got dressed.

We arrived at the party ten minutes later and I ordered Sue and myself soft drinks, which seemed to please her.

As we stood there sipping our drinks, I spotted the manager. I excused myself, wishing to speak to him in private. Sue seemed to understand, so I went to the manager and introduced myself, "I need to talk to you for a moment, if you don't mind, sir?"

"I don't mind. You have a complaint?"

"No, this place and the service has been exemplary." We now walked to an empty corner where I inquired, "How old does a girl have to be before becoming a prostitute in a bar? And question two, how old to drink in bars?"

He chuckled informing me, "If that's the problem, you don't have one. There is no age limit for either." He must have sensed my confusion, for he explained, "Girls have to weigh sixty-five pounds or more to be working girls and to drink in bars. The top of their head must be above the counter. Does that put your mind at rest?"

"You bet it does. Thank you. If you will please excuse me now, I must get back to my girl." We shook hands as he nodded. Then I went back to Sue and asked her, "You ready to go?" She was, so setting our drinks aside, we left.

Back in my room, we undressed and went to bed. I was glad to have Sue to myself with nothing else planned, except what we were going to do together between now and when I had to leave in the morning.

The next morning we showered together, kissing a lot and I had so many questions. This girl seemed different than the ones I had met in the past. She was certainly more beautiful. But more than that, she made me feel special and content. I asked, "How much does it cost to feed a family here?"

"A family of four can live on two American dollars and fifty cents a day. That covers food, rent, utilities, and clothes."

That was beyond my comprehension, so I inquired further, "What is your general tradition on marriage?"

"Husband make money, wife stays home taking care of house, husband, and children. Husband have right to enjoy himself at home as well as in town, with or without wife."

"You mean the husband is allowed to have other girls even after he's married?"

She told me very seriously, "Oh yes, even at home."

Thinking she was joking, I remarked playfully, "Yeah, we just put out the red light and start a line."

She told me very seriously, "You don't understand. Say you and I marry and at home. You see pretty girl you want. So you tell me. I go bargain with her. If she says yes, I bring her into our home and after fixing supper for us, you and her go to bed, I sleep in other..."

I interrupted, "And you're okay with this happening?"

She answered, laying a hand against the side of my face, "It a tradition and I very traditional girl. You rather me be different?" I shook my head and she continued, "I sleep on couch, the next morning, after breakfast, I take her outside and pay her, then she leaves."

As she stopped and watched me, I assumed for a reaction. I

was thinking it sounded like a good idea for the guy as I inquired, "Does the same thing go for the wife?"

"No! If wife caught with other man, she disgrace family. She go to the Temple and after ceremony, kill herself."

I thought this a little drastic, but kind of liked the concept as I asked, hoping I wasn't going too far, "How old were you when you started this kind of work?"

She astonished me beyond belief with, "We are taught as young girl to please a man. Papa make sure we are ready before we leave home to be on our own."

She took a breath and I broke in, raising my voice, "You mean your father is the first to have sex with you and ..."

I fell silent not knowing what to say next. She caressed the side of my face explaining, "It is his right, honey. He paid to raise me, so first time his right. But only that time. Then we leave to work in massage parlor. That is the way with girls' life in this country."

This was too much for me. So I left the other questions alone, afraid the answers to them may shock me even more than I was now. Laying on the bed, I held her in my arms tenderly, never wanting to let her go.

Soon Sue said softly, but not moving, "We going to have to leave soon."

We kissed some more before getting up and dressing. Then we headed for the elevator, taking our things with us.

After breakfast, Sue handed me a piece of paper. I opened it and found her full name and address. I looked at her as she informed me, "I like you. If you come back, would you stay with me at my home? That way you save money. But in the meantime, could we write each other?"

I was delighted at both suggestions. I answered quickly, "I'd like to take you in my arms to answer both questions. But yes, I would consider it an honor to write such a precious lady. And I will be back, count on it."

It was time for Sue to go. I took what money I had left after paying for breakfast, it came to a couple Baht and I handed it to her saying, "It isn't much, but use this to get home. It won't do me any good. I just wish it was a hundred times more."

She shook her head shoving my hand with the money in it away saying, "You keep it, I have money, but thank you." I put the money in my pocket as Sue shocked me by kissing me on the lips in public and I didn't care. It felt good. But before I could reach out, she parted our lips and rushed from the restaurant. I watched her with a blank mind, sadness sweeping over me. So I sat down and ordered a coke while I waited.

A Sergeant came in looking around. Seeing me sitting alone, he came to the table and asked, "You mind if I wait with you soldier?" I shook my head, but not speaking and he sat down, introducing himself, "I'm Sergeant Sellers. What's your name?"

I just answered, "Weaver." Figuring by my insignia on my uniform he would know my rank. I didn't feel like talking.

We shook hands and then he pulled out a fifth of whiskey from his bag that was about a third full. He sat it on the table remarking, "Leaving them is the hardest part. Would you help me kill this poor thing? It's suffering tremendously. So let's put it out of its misery and ours to rest. And if this bottle isn't enough for ours, I have its twin sister in my bag, too."

I called to the waitress, "Two large cokes, please Miss."

We finished off the bottle and was well into the other when

the bus arrived. We staggered onto it, found two seats together and commenced trying to finish off the bottle.

At the Air Field, we sat on the bus, waiting for our flight. Suddenly, I had to pee real bad, but we had been ordered to stay aboard the bus which had no restroom in it.

I told Sergeant Sellers of my problem and he reminded me of our orders to stay put. I replied, "I either go out there or right here in the seat."

I got up the best I could as he told me, "If you go in the building, they'll catch you."

I steadied myself and then headed down the aisle in silence. I soon found myself at the open door of the bus and feeling I had no other choice, I opened the fly of my pants and began peeing on the sidewalk outside, not caring who or how many people passed by getting splashed on. But people seeing what I was doing gave the door a wide detour.

When I finished, I zipped up my pants, made my way back to the seat and sat down, telling Sergeant Sellers, "I didn't get off the bus." Then I took possession of the bottle for another drink.

The time came and with help, I made it aboard the plane. The engines started and I could feel the plane moving. I waited anxiously for the take-off, the best part of the ride for me. The plane lurched forward heading down the runway, then we were off the ground, climbing, and climbing, and climbing.

I opened my eyes wondering where I was. Everything was still and quiet. I was in a bed. That much I knew, but how and where? And most of all, when did that damn plane level off.

I had apparently landed at Da Nang, got another plane to Chu

Lai, caught a ride to the company, got undressed and climbed into my own bed, remembering nothing.

I got up and dressed, figuring Sellers had been instrumental in my arriving here.

After breakfast, I headed for the lumber yard. Ron sat in my office, cooling in front of my fan and I asked him, "Did everything go smoothly while I was gone?"

Ron answered, "Like glass. How was your R & R?"

I told him all about it and finished by asking, as I looked around, "Where are the workers?"

"The day after you left, the workers were laid off due to the upcoming Tet Offensive. Too many of them were turning out to be VC"

I dismissed it and remarked, "Well, I guess you'd like to get going? So I'll take it from here."

He said yes and was off down the road. I headed for the Conex containing my souvenir weapons.

They were as I left them, so I went back to the office and put all the entries into my ledger Ron had kept as I had instructed.

After lunch, I went to the Radio Shack and asked Dan, the Company Radio Operator, "You keeping in communication with my squad out in the bush?"

Dan told me, "Not much today. Yesterday, they were pinned down for several hours. But no casualties. Other than that, it's been real quiet. So how was your R & R?"

"Great, I'll tell you all about it later. Right now, who's RTO (Radio Technical Operator) today?"

Dan looked at his watch and then told me, "Right now it should be your buddy Don."

"Could you get him on the radio so I can let him know I'm back?"

Dan keyed the mike and spoke into it, "Lone Wolf, this is Home Lamb, come in. Over." Then he released the button, waited a moment and when there wasn't a response, he repeated it all again.

This time a voice came back, "Home Lamb, this is Lone Wolf. Come in. Over."

Dan keyed the mike again and announced, "Lone Wolf, someone's here to say hi, unless you got something going? Over."

I didn't recognize Don's voice coming over the radio, but when the voice said, "Put the lazy good for nothing on. Over." I knew it was Don and Dan handed me the mike.

I keyed the mike declaring, "Hi buddy. How's it going out there? Keeping your head down? Over."

Don chuckled over the mike answering, "So far, but how in the hell was your vacation? Over."

"Come back in and find out over a beer. Course, you're buying because I'm broke. Over."

Don laughed over the speaker before he interjected, "Okay, just keep em cold, should be back ..." The speaker went dead.

Dan took the mike speaking into it, "Come in Lone Wolf, this is Home Lamb. Over." When there was no reply, he went through the procedure several times before telling me, "His batteries could be dead. If they come back on line, I'll let you know."

I thanked him and left, heading for my Hooch, knowing that at least Don knew I was back and he was okay.

There wasn't anything for me to worry about, so getting my gear, I headed for the lumber yard and found three people in a jeep waiting for me. The driver was a Corporal. In the passenger's seat a Major and in the back a First Lieutenant.

I saluted, then as both officers returned my salute, I said, "May I help you, Sir?" I was directing my question to the Major.

The Major got out, followed by the others and he told me, "We're from S-1 and I must say you have been doing a great job here. We've come down to see how you do it. No one else has ever been able to run things as smoothly. Shall we have a look around?"

I replied proudly, "Thank you, Sir. Everything is in order for your inspection."

As I showed them around explaining my procedure, the Corporal wrote on his clipboard. First I showed them my office where the Corporal went through my ledger. Then we spent the next half hour counting units of lumber, then sandbags and everything balanced to my ledger.

I saved the Conex's for last, starting with the one closest to my office. When I opened the door to the last one, I explained, "These are my extra sandbags. When a load comes in short, I add to it from this and when over, I put the extras in here for later. That's why my ledgers and materials balance." I hoped that was enough to satisfy the Major.

But apparently not, because he spoke over his shoulder stepping into the Conex, "That's fine and a good way to handle things. Let's have a look. "The first bundle he picked up revealed the barrels of the weapons. Looking back at me, he asked, "What have we here?"

I now figured that Ron had given me up. There was no sense in making excuses, so I stepped in beside the Major and spoke up, "Well Sir, before I went on R & R, a Vietnamese Lieutenant and his men came in to get sandbags, having the proper paperwork. After they were gone, I discovered their weapons had been left behind. I put them in here and went on R & R, figuring to deal with it when I got back. I just got back and have to wait for the Lieutenant or his men to return, so..."

I stopped hoping I had stretched the truth enough to where the Major believed me.

The Major stood there a moment, studying me. Then he said, "I'll accept that story soldier. But if they don't come back within a week, I'd better not find these automatics anywhere around here. The AK-44 you may keep as a war souvenir, as long as you register it with supply. Is that understood?"

I replied, "Yes Sir, perfectly." And without another word, he dropped the bundle and left the Conex with me right behind him.

At the jeep, we saluted and they drove off, not looking back. I felt relieved that I wouldn't get into trouble as long as I got rid of all but the weapon designated, so I locked up everything and called it a day.

The next morning, I decided to get my AK-44 registered, so I took it to supply, where Gary looked it over before saying, "I'll give you two hundred dollars for it?"

"Sorry, Gary, but it's not for sale. I just need to register it with you."

"Four hundred? I can't go any higher?"

I apologized, "I'm sorry, but it's not for sale buddy. I need to take it home for my father. He's a gun collector and this may get me the recognition from him that I have been trying to get all my life."

"How did you get it?"

I gave him the same story I'd given the Major. When finished, Gary shrugged and took out the paperwork. He filled it out and I signed it. Then Gary got a box that the rifle would fit into perfectly. He attached the paper to the box, then informed me, "I'll have to keep it here until you're ready to go home."

I knew he was right, but announced, "Okay, but I'm holding you personally responsible. If it vanishes, my M-16 and I won't be forgiving. Understand, this is not a threat, for I like you. But you'd do the same thing if the shoe was on the other foot."

Gary responded grinning and nodding, "Yeah, I'd do the same. Don't worry, it'll be here when you're ready to go home."

I went back to my office and a few minutes later, a jeep pulled up. It was Sergeant Holt. I greeted him with, "Hi Sarg. It's been long time no see."

Sergeant Holt replied as we shook hands, "I was around a few days ago, but you were gone. I thought you had quit."

"I was on R & R." And I gave him the highlights of it and he listened intensely.

When I finished, he explained, "I hate to ask, but I really need some sandbags again and as usual I can't..."

I interrupted with, "Just bring your men in and get em. To

hell with paperwork." Sergeant Holt thanked me and was off, only to be back ten minutes later with three men.

As his men gathered their bundles, I told Holt, "I have a big problem that you may be able to help me with."

Sergeant Holt answered seriously, "Who do you need killed?"

I laughed before informing him, "No, nothing like that. Here's my problem." I moved the couple bundles that revealed the weapons.

As Sergeant Holt stared at the rifles, I gave him the story I had given the others, finishing with, "I need to get rid of these before the Major comes back. Would you and your men be interested in taking them off my hands?"

Sergeant Holt quickly replied, "I'll give you fifty ..."

I waved him off explaining, "I didn't say anything about selling them. I have to get them out of here. If you and your men want em, they're free."

"Consider them gone and be assured, they will be put to good use." Then he and his men, still carrying two bundles apiece, picked up a weapon each as well. Then they rushed off, I figured they did so before I could recant.

The next day, the company came back while I was in the Hooch getting ready for work. But only Cole, Mike, and John came in. So I asked, "Where's Don?"

Cole looked at the others, then at me inquiring, "You didn't hear?" I shook my head, feeling a cold chill go through me as he went on, "Don got hit. He was RTO a few days ago when Ralph stepped on a land mine, killing himself and Jay, who was walking between Ralph and Don. Don and Bob took shrapnel, but still they were alive when they were choppered out. Other than that, I don't know anything else." I was on my feet, heading out the door without comment.

Outside, I ran to the radio room, where I asked Dan, in as controlled a voice as possible, "Please find out what hospital Don's in for me, please?" Dan stared at me and I explained what Cole had told me.

Obviously not knowing anything about it, when I fell silent, Dan quickly got on the radio. I wasn't paying any attention to what he was doing or saying. My mind was thinking about Don.

Soon Dan told me, "Don's okay. He took three pieces of shrapnel in the chest. But they say he now just needs a few days rest and then they'll send him back."

I let out a sigh of relief and told Dan, "Thanks, I owe you big time." And I left.

I walked back to my Hooch. Hatred growing even more so inside me. I knew that somehow, I would be shown the way to kill the VC for hurting Don.

Back in the Hooch, I told the guys what I had found out about Don. Then I noticed Tim wasn't in either. So I asked, "Where's Tim?"

Mike spoke this time, "He didn't make it either. He bought it yesterday by a sniper at the LZ (Landing Zone). Just as we were being picked up. "

I asked, "Was the sniper gotten?"

The guys looked at each other chuckling before Mike told me, "Oh yeah! He was dead before he hit the ground from his perch in the tree. No one stopped firing until he landed on the ground. I even have his ears. You want to see em?" He picked up his pack and dug into it. I walked over to Mike as he pulled them out. I had never seen detached ears before. I didn't know what to say as I looked at them.

A few days later, I saw Don in a jeep, being brought home from the hospital. I bolted from my office, meeting him almost before he had completely gotten out of the jeep, asking, "How are you feeling?"

Shaking hands Don answered, "Fine. A little sore, but okay."

Now I told him, in a joking manner, "Hey! If you didn't want to talk to me on the radio, all you had to do was say so. You didn't have to try and get yourself killed to get out of paying for the beer."

"You went on a vacation! I needed one, too, and the nurses made it all worthwhile. They were great."

As we walked to the Hooch, I started telling him about my vacation. I continued while he laid down on his cot, finishing with, "When you go on your R & R, why don't you just go ahead and shoot me, so I can find out how yours was? But right now, you get some rest." He nodded and I left.

It was supper-time before I saw Don again. As we sat eating, Don informed me, "When I reported in this morning, they said we're going out in the morning. It's going to be rougher than usual, due to the 'Tet Offensive' starting."

This was the second time I'd heard that term used. I inquired about it, "What's this 'Tet Offensive' I keep hearing about?"

"I asked the same question and was told that it's the Vietnamese New Year. It's celebrated from the last week in January through the first week of February for it lasts for a few weeks."

"But New Year's was several weeks ago. Why are they running so late with theirs?"

"I was told this is the time of year when the Vietnamese having been storing up rockets and mortars for several months. They'll use this period of time to hit us with everything they have."

"WOW!" I said, then I took a bite of food before stating, "You know, I've been here all these months and I still haven't seen a rice paddy up close, not like you have."

"I thought you said if your children ever ask what you did in the war, you wanted to be able to tell them you never left the lumber yard. Why the change of mind now? "

I laughed a little before answering, "I didn't say I wanted to go out and lose the lumber yard. I just want to look around for a day and then come back." I didn't realize that my words would come back to haunt me. The subject changed to my telling him about the weapons and my war souvenir.

We finished eating and left, heading back to the Hooch where we laid around, trying to figure out what we wanted to do next.

Sergeant Hicks came in and walked directly up to me laying on my cot. He said, "Weaver. Get your gear together. You're going out with your squad in the morning."

I jumped up quickly asking, "I am? What about the ..."

He interrupted with, "It's all arranged. Ron Shapard is taking over the lumber yard."

Puzzled, I inquired, "May I ask why this has come about?"

Sergeant Hicks smiled answering, "It's simple really. I was sitting behind you in the mess hall earlier, talking to Alfred. I overheard you talking about wanting to go out. Well, we need men out there. So, Weaver, I arranged for you to get your wish. Square your stuff from the office and be prepared to go out in the morning, at 0600 hours. The guys will help you pack. So you're not carrying stuff you don't need." Then he turned to leave the Hooch.

I stood there stuttering, "But ... but ... but." And the door closed behind him.

I looked at Don laying on his cot. He was holding his stomach, he was laughing so hard. But no sound was coming from him.

As he calmed down, he looked at me, opening his mouth to speak. But before he could utter a word, he burst out laughing again, but this time not quietly as he rolled back and forth on his cot. I wished he would roll off the bed. I finally spoke spitefully, "Oh, screw you!" Then I stormed out of the Hooch slamming the door behind me. But that just enhanced Don's laughter.

* * *

* * *

I went to the office and collected my things. Then arriving back in the Hooch, I found Don in control of himself. I asked him, "You done?"

Don exclaimed, "I'm sorry buddy. But you have to admit its funny how this worked out. You did want to go out and see what it was like and now you will."

I smiled knowing he was right and replied, "Yeah, I know. But damn, I didn't want to lose the lumber yard all together."

"I know and I am sorry. But he was right. We do need you out there. Besides, it's not all that bad."

I shrugged responding, "How about helping me pack so I don't overdo it?"

Soon we had my pack loaded. Besides a change of socks and underwear, it contained twenty-five one-pound bricks of C-4 (Plastic Explosives), three fragmentation grenades, five percussion grenades and a pair of earplugs.

I packed my raincoat and rain pants too, though Don tried to talk me out of bringing them. But with the monsoons coming, I was taking them. Along with an entrenching tool (shovel) and a compass, I added in a few C-rations, and then I rolled up my sleeping bag tying it underneath the pack.

I sat the pack on the floor, draped several bandoleers of ammunition over it, and then equipped my pistol belt with the twenty-six filled ammunition clips I had collected along the way, each having in them eighteen rounds. To my belt, I added a bayonet and a wooden probing knife. Lastly, I laid my M-16, flak jacket, gas mask, and helmet on top of all this. I was now ready to go. Don told me that anything else I may need, someone would have it brought out to me.

I learned we were going out on the Chu Lai Peninsula, but that was all the information I could find out.

We all went to bed early and was back up by the break of dawn. We had breakfast and by 0600, we were standing in front of the CO's office with Sergeant Hicks addressing us, "Intelligence tells us that two Divisions of North Vietnamese, hard-core regulars, are building to mount an offensive from the peninsula. Two divisions have been made up of Engineers, Mobile Cavalry and Infantry. Our objective will be to drive them to the end of the peninsula, where the USS New Jersey will pound the beach with their sixteen-inch guns. Are there any questions?" When there wasn't any, he added, "Okay then. Load up."

We climbed onto the backs of the trucks and soon we were speeding down Highway One.

We stopped at a large landing pad with helicopters on it. They were for moving troops and were called "Gunships." Eight men and their gear could be loaded onto each chopper.

Being the last man to climb aboard ours, I sat on the floor at the open door. Soon the engines started and got louder and louder as the rotor's turned faster and faster. Suddenly, it's tail rose first and then the whole thing followed and I was going up in my first helicopter ride.

I could see everything from up there as the choppers flew in formation over water for a while, then over land with square rice paddies bordered by small dikes.

Don leaned against me, and pointing at the ground, shouted so I could hear him over the sound of the engines, "There's your rice paddies buddy." I just smiled at him and nodded.

I continued watching the scenery change below as we flew over dense forest land. Now and then an opening appeared, some having villages in them, the people looking like large ants.

We landed in an opening that would only hold three choppers at a time. As the first three touched down, we bailed out and they quickly rose letting three more come in and there were now literally dozens of these choppers flying in the area.

Once men and gear were on the ground, we formed around Sergeant Hicks who announced, "We'll hook up with the other units soon. For now, spread out and keep an eye open. Stay in line and watch your intervals. Now move out!" And at the edge of the trees, everyone spread out and we entered slowly.

After several hundred meters, the forest opened again and sitting around were hundreds, maybe even thousands of men.

Armored Personnel Carriers (APC's) were spread out among them.

Among the APC's there were tanks that fired ninety-millimeter rounds from their torrents' long barrels. As we stood there in the hot sun, waiting to be told what to do as sweat ran down our bodies, I took in everything I could.

My backpack alone weighed about sixty pounds when we left camp. But now it felt like it weighed at least two hundred pounds!

Soon Sergeant Hicks announced, "Form up into groups of four. Weaver. You being the new guy, stay with me."

I turned to Don asking, "You and I together?"

He nodded and then Cole came over and asked, "Can I join you two?" Don and I nodded.

Once the groups were formed, Sergeant Hicks told us, "Okay now, each group attach yourselves to an APC..." Then, looking at us, he continued, "You three and I will be with that one." And he pointed to the APC at the end of the line, closest to us putting us on the far right end of the line.

We followed him to the back of the APC where we all took our packs off as Sergeant Hicks suggested, "If you don't want to carry your packs, hang them on the back of the APC like this." He hung his on the back of the track finishing with, "This way you can get to them easily whether you are walking or riding."

We duplicated what he did and then went to the nearby trees. We sat down in the shade, awaiting further orders.

While we sat in the shade and waited, I surveyed the line of vehicles parked along one edge of the clearing. There were fifteen vehicles in all: three APC's with a fifty-caliber machine gun mounted on the top front of the machine and a sixty-caliber machine gun mounted on each side.

Then there was a tank with a ninety-millimeter cannon and a fifty-caliber on top, then there were three APC's and it was this way for the whole line.

I also saw that each APC and tank had a five man crew.

About half an hour later, Sergeant Hicks told us, "If you don't want to walk, get on board."

Don, Cole, and I climbed on top, sitting with our legs hanging over the back of the APC. Sergeant Hicks positioned himself on top of the APC, behind the mounted fifty-caliber.

As the vehicles moved forward, the men on all the mounted machine guns intently focused upon the distance of their respective side of the APC's.

The engines roared to life and they were so loud, we couldn't talk to each other without yelling.

As the vehicles moved out, it wasn't the most comfortable way to travel, but it beat walking. It was also very slow going, but steady.

Several lines of infantrymen followed the tracks and it reminded me of a movie set, but this time I was part of it.

We hadn't gone far when suddenly a shot was heard over the sound of the engines. The APC's immediately stopped and the three of us bailed off the back of it.

The Cavalrymen and Sergeant Hicks stayed behind their mounted weapons.

Everyone on the ground stayed behind the vehicles where it was safe, not knowing from where the shot had come.

More shots rang out, but I couldn't tell who was shooting. It was beginning to get rather heavy with automatic weapon fire from the APC's joining in.

I knelt, thinking, 'Well, I'm finally in the thick of things.' And then I quickly peeked around the corner of the vehicle to see if I could spot any movement.

The ground around us was mostly sand. Small sprays of it started kicking up close to me as bullets began hitting it. Then I saw the muzzle flash from the weapon causing them and I jerked my head back to safety. I prepared to put my weapon around the corner and fire when all the shooting stopped just as suddenly as it had begun.

The Infantry moved out ahead of the vehicles to check the wooded area for more snipers, but there was no more shooting and soon we were moving again with the infantrymen moving back behind the vehicles.

The rest of the day was slow. Every now and then I could hear a shot ring out, but nothing that stopped our moving forward.

When we stopped for the night, Sergeant Hicks inquired, "I need a volunteer. It seems the Vietnamese like to sneak up after dark and turn our Claymore's around on us. So I need someone to booby trap them with a little surprise. Any takers?"

Don had been explaining the hit and run method to me. So what the Sergeant was asking seemed to me a way of getting back, so I said, "I might as well get my feet wet. I'll go." I didn't know how literally that expression would be this time.

After dark, I found myself laying in about twelve inches of rice paddy water, placing Claymore's in it with a grenade underneath, below water level. I held the Claymore down against the handle of the grenade while I pulled the pin of the grenade. Then I eased my hand off the Claymore, until I could release it all together hoping it wouldn't move. Then I moved onto the next one.

When I was finished, I knew that if anyone raised one of the Claymore's, just an inch, it would be the last time they raised anything.

I was completely wet yet, but the night was so warm, I would dry fast. I reported the job done before going to my sleeping bag and crawled in, wet clothes and all.

The next morning we were up and by daybreak, I had retrieved the Claymore's and grenades. We climbed aboard the APC's as before and were on our way.

The noise of the engines didn't seem as loud today for some reason. But we still had to yell to hear each other as the APC's moved in line again. The Infantry fell in behind us and again it looked like a scene from a World War II movie script.

Along about noon, the APC we rode on found itself separated from the rest of the column. We were on a dirt road with a very thick forest of trees and brush lining both sides of the road.

We stopped and the engine went dead. Sergeant Hicks called down to the driver with anger in his voice, "Where in the hell are you taking us? For a Sunday drive? Can't you see there's no other APC's around?"

The driver replied, "The road was here and it seemed to be going in the same direction we were headed. I thought..."

Sergeant Hicks interrupted him, very loud and angrily. I thought any second Hicks would jump inside the APC and strangle the driver. "Stop thinking and pull your head out of your ass. Look around once in a while. You'll see that we're lost and alone in the middle of nowhere. So if you don't get us back pronto, I'm sticking this fifty up your ass and I'll empty a belt. You understand me, soldier?"

One of the cavalrymen added, "And I'll help him, Sam!"

The engine started and the vehicle lurched forward heading down the road. We all looked for a way through the trees to our left. But about a hundred meters more and the road made a sharp turn to the right. We came to a sudden stop because there was a tree laying across the road. The engine died again.

The driver called up, "What now, Sergeant?"

Sergeant Hicks answered, "Turn around dumbass and go back to where we got separated. Hopefully, we'll catch up to them."

The engine started and we turned around, heading back. I smiled and yelled to Don, "Looks like we're either trying to avoid the war or find one of our own."

Don called back, "We'd better hope it's the first." I nodded, completely agreeing with him.

About two-thirds of the way back, another tree lay across the road. The APC stopped and the engine went dead. Sergeant Hicks shouted, "Heads up! Ambush situation!" And our senses went on full alert as we scanned the area while pulling our backpacks upon the APC with us.

When nothing happened for a few minutes, the engine started up again and we turned around heading back the way we had come.

The ligaments in the back of my legs started hurting. I decided to pull my legs up, putting them under me. I yelled over to Don and Cole after finding they were having the same problem, "One-two-three, we'll all sit Indian-style, okay?" Both smiled, nodding. So I yelled, "ONE!" Together in unison, the three of us rolled back on top of the APC, raising our legs high into the air over our heads. At that moment, the world seemed to erupt as an explosion deafened us. The back of the APC jumped up into the air, we had run over a land mine.

The word ambush filled my thoughts as my training took over. Before the dust even started to settle, the three of us, with our weapons, lay prone on the ground behind the APC watching our own field of fire.

Soon the dust settled and I wondered why we hadn't been fired upon yet? This was nothing like what we had been taught.

After a while, I turned to evaluate the damage to the APC. On the side I had been sitting on, the treads had been blown off and now lay on the ground. It didn't look serious, so I rolled back on my belly and scanned my area of vision waiting for a target to appear.

I don't know how much time passed before three APC's came bursting through the trees and brush. I didn't hear them, but I felt the ground shaking as they appeared. Then I realized I couldn't hear anything. The explosion had deafened me.

I saw Hicks and some men from the other APC's dismount and meet together to talk. I was frustrated over having fought so hard to get where I was and one explosion destroyed it all.

Someone tapped me on the shoulder, startling me. Looking, I didn't recognize him. He shouted and I could barely hear him. I was at least thankful for that, "It's over. You can get up now." I got up, figuring maybe my hearing would come back and I wouldn't have to report it. I stood, watching the APC crews inspecting our damaged craft. My hearing did start to slowly return because I was able to now hear a little bit more of the conversation.

A Captain appeared and started looking the situation over while Sergeant Hicks explained what had happened.

The guy who told me all was clear, came back to tell me, "Your hearing will come back completely soon. Don't worry, it happens to everyone that goes through that kind of experience."

I nodded, hoping he was right as he walked away.

I pushed the palm of my hands against my ears really hard and then pulled them away quickly. My hearing seemed even clearer.

One of the guys had gotten a pry bar and was trying to bend the piece of metal that worked as a fender for the APC, out of the gears for the tread. Unfortunately, he was failing miserably.

I could see that the blast had come up the back of the APC right under the spot I had been sitting. I told Don and Cole, who were now standing close by, "Damn, are we ever lucky? A minute longer and I, for one, wouldn't have any legs. And to think, we were just horse-playing around."

Cole commented, "You only have eight more to go, Ward." And I knew he was comparing me to a cat's nine lives.

I responded, "What about you two?"

Don spoke now, "You were directly over it Ward. We might have lost our legs, but you would have lost a whole lot more." A chill ran through me, knowing he was probably right.

"Damn it, it won't budge!" The angry voice brought my attention back to the APC, seeing it was the guy with the bar that was frustrated.

I remarked, "I can get that out with no sweat."

The Captain replied, "Do it, soldier." I got a brick of C-4 out of my pack and as I peeled the adhesive off one side and placed it on top of the fender, the Captain asked, "You going to blow it off?"

I answered, smiling, "No, I 'm just going to heat it up so it'll bend easier."

As I lit my lighter, I looked around and everyone but Don, Cole, and Sergeant Hicks had vanished. These three, however, had backed way away from the APC, several feet. I asked them, "Where did everyone go?"

As Don and Cole chuckled, a voice from behind a tree answered, "You can blow yourself up. We're not taking any chances." Then I lit the C-4.

Basic facts about C-4: It needs a blasting cap to make it explode. But you can set it on fire safely and it burns with no visible flame, odor or smoke as it slowly disintegrates. But it burns white hot. I knew it would heat the metal fender enough to make it pliable so I could easily bend it back out of the tread gear. However, the downside to this is that if a piece of the burning C-4 was hit with something, or if it should fall off the fender and hit the ground ... Well, let's just say my other eight "cat" lives Cole said I still had, would rapidly be used up! The explosion would result in my total obliteration.

As I watched it burn, I heard Sergeant Hicks comment, "We sure have a lot of chickens around here." He started clucking like a chicken and I looked back to see him with his arms folded, his hands under his armpits, flapping his elbows like wings.

A voice now exclaimed, "And where were you going when he lit it?" And there was a loud chorus of laughter all around.

Sergeant Hicks replied, heading for the trees, "To take a piss. You mind?" And looking my way, he gave me a smiling wink.

I went back to watching the C-4 turn the fender almost white hot hoping none of the C-4 would fall off the fender as I took a pair of pliers and tried to pull the fender out of the gear, but couldn't.

Sergeant Hicks having returned said, "Cole, get your pliers and help him." With Cole's help, we finally straightened out the fender. We held it in place as it cooled down to where we could release it. Then getting a canteen, I poured the water on the fender to finish cooling it off.

Once Cole and I were out of the way, it didn't take the APC crew long to have the tread back on. Then we boarded our ride and following the other APC's back through the trees and brush.

At one point a limb almost swept us off the APC, but we soon burst out into an opening where men sat around waiting for us. The APC's we followed now joined the line where they had been before coming to our rescue. Our APC moved in line where we were supposed to be and turned its engine off. We dismounted and relaxed for a bit.

After what seemed like just a few minutes, everyone loaded back up and we got ready to move out. In front of us, I could see several rice paddies, each square bordered by a small dike. The Captain atop one of the tanks, made a circular motion with his arm over his head and when it went out before him, men and machines moved out in that direction.

After going about half a mile without incident, we came to a stop and everyone got down to stretch their legs.

I didn't see where Don and Cole vanished to as Sergeant Hicks approached me and asked, "Is it true you like blowing things up?" I nodded and he went on, "Well then, have I got a job for you. Get eight Bangalore Torpedo's and follow me."

From inside the APC, I retrieved eight of the six-foot length round pipes that were about four inches in diameter, which one can be connected to the others to blow up lines through wire or mine fields.

I followed Hicks to two long rows of coiled barbed wire spread out on the ground with a row of it on top of these.

Now Sergeant Hicks told me, "We need at least a ten-foot wide section of this taken out and cleared of possible land mines. Can you do it?"

"Piece of cake," I replied and Sergeant Hicks walked off as I set to work connecting four of the pipes together and slid them under the wires.

After setting the blasting caps and fuses, I lit both. Then I made my way to an APC, yelling out three times, "FIRE IN THE HOLE!"

After it went off, I asked Sergeant Hicks, "Anything else needing to be blown up?"

He answered, "We have wells to blow up."

I shrugged. "Let's go," I said.

Sergeant Hicks instructed me to get two shaped-charges. I went into the APC and got two 'forty pounders' and then followed Hicks to the first well, which was full of water.

I sat the charges on the ground next to the well and found a sturdy limb, which I placed across the opening of the well.

A shaped-charges power is directed more outward, than up or down. I grabbed a roll of Det-cord (a fuse that is an explosive itself) and cut off about a ten-foot length. I tied one end to the charge and the other to the middle of the limb. Then I lowered the charge into the well.

I set the blasting cap to the end of the Det-cord tied to the limb. Hicks yelled out three times, "FIRE IN THE HOLE." I lit the fuse and headed for a tree to hide behind.

It went off, spraying us with water, even behind the tree. I suddenly remembered the other charge I'd laid beside the well.

When I was able to look, I did and saw it had gone off as well.

After retrieving another from the APC, this time I placed the blasting cap and fuse directly on the charge. I tied a ten-foot piece of twine to the charge and the other end to another limb laid across the opening. I lit the fuse as Hicks yelled, "FIRE IN THE HOLE!" three times and I lowered the charge into the water before heading for a tree.

From behind the tree, I looked to see where Hicks was hiding.

148

I didn't see him until I looked around the area and saw him still at the well. He was leaning over it, looking down into the water. I figured he was watching the fuse burn.

I called out, "You'd better get out of there." But he just waved me off, never looking up from the water. I knew there wasn't much time left as he suddenly bolted from the well, diving behind a stump as the well exploded.

I pulled my head back behind the tree as the blast threw water everywhere.

The last well was out away from everything by itself and it was empty. There were tunnels going in two different directions at the bottom of it.

I was told to open the well so the tunnel could be checked out. I looked it over and assessed that two shaped-charges placed a third of the way down would, or should, do the job. I set to work assembling the explosives, blasting cap and fuses.

As I started to light the fuse, the limb broke and I cursed.

I wasn't sure what to do. Finally, I took a brick of C-4, put a blasting cap and fuse to it and lit it, dropping it into the well and headed across the field for cover yelling, "FIRE IN THE HOLE!"

I hoped it would open the well as desired rather than collapsing the tunnels.

After it went off, I inspected the well. Neither the tunnel, nor the well, made out of brick, was affected by the blast.

Sergeant Hicks came overlooking the well over and shook his head commenting, "I've never seen one this stubborn. I wonder how we are going to open it up."

I had an idea. But I figured he would reject it as I said, If I had an ounce of Nitro, it should do the job."

Sergeant Hicks just remarked, "You got it!" And walked away, leaving me wondering if he was serious.

Half an hour later, a chopper came in and landed. Sergeant Hicks told me, pointing at the chopper, "There's your Nitro! But you're on your own!" And he headed off across the field to join everyone else.

The helicopter had landed close to me and the nitroglycerin had been transported in a small box, about six inches square.

Carefully, I slowly took the box across the field to the well as the chopper took off.

I opened the box and took the vial out. The vial contained one fluid ounce of the explosive oil.

I wrapped Det-cord around it and wrapped duct tape around the Det-cord to make sure the vial didn't slip out. I tied the other end of the cord to a limb I'd placed across the opening. Then I lowered the vial into the well.

Giving myself an extra-long fuse. I lit it and took off, running across the field as fast as I could run, yelling as loud as I could, "FIRE IN THE HOLE!"

When it went off, though I'd made it a good hundred meters or more away, dust, dirt and small pieces of brick sprayed the area. It caused everyone to scurry for cover.

Once everything settled down, Sergeant Hicks and I went to check it out. We found the well open as I figured. But both tunnels had collapsed and Sergeant Hicks told me, "I kind of thought you were over-doing it, but I wanted you to find out for yourself and now you know that not always are bigger blasts better."

I nodded, commenting, "I said it 'Should' do the job and I was half right." I walked away expecting him to yell at me, but he didn't.

For the next few days, we only moved ten miles at a time. I blew up many wells, some wire and a few old Bunkers left behind by the French when they were here before America got involved.

My favorite was the deserted villages. I was able to place a shaped-charge inside each hut, then ran Det-cord from around one, out the door to the inside of the next and around that charge. I kept doing this until I had the charges in every structure connected by a single Det-cord. Then when I set off the blasting cap at one end, the whole village instantly went up in one beautiful explosion.

One morning, Sergeant Hicks approached me. "I have another job for you, Weaver. One you should really like," he said.

The way he said it, I was skeptical, but without any questions I picked up my gear and followed him to a cave at the base of a small mountain where he said, "There it is, you're training as a 'Tunnel Rat' aren't you'? Well go in and check it out!"

I was trained as such. But being six-foot-three inches tall and weighing a hundred and eighty-five pounds, I had never thought I'd be called upon to perform this function. But here I was. I handed Hicks my gear, took his forty-five caliber pistol and put my earplugs in, took out a percussion grenade and pulled the pin tossing it inside the cave as far as I could.

We all stepped aside until after it went off, tripping any booby-traps, and killing all snakes staked inside for a ways. The snakes were one of Charlie's favorite tricks.

I picked up my flashlight and wooden probe knife and entered the cave.

I went as far inside as I figured the grenade had cleared out. I started poking the probe-knife gently into the ground feeling for land-mines or other instruments of destruction.

Traveling was slow, probing every inch in front of me. An hour later, I figured I'd moved maybe a hundred feet. I sat down relaxing my muscles, which ached from being tense for so long. I finally said, "To hell with this!" Leaving my knife to mark where I'd stopped, I exited the cave to get an explosive charge.

No one asked my intentions as I reentered the cave with my charge.

I stopped where my knife was left and then attaching a fuse and blasting cap, I called out, "If anyone is in here, you better De-De-Mow or in a moment you won't be able to."

Getting no response, and having given myself plenty of fuse, I lit it and exited the cave. I spoke in a normal voice, "Fire in the hole."

The charge went off while Sergeant Hicks and I headed back to our APC as I thought, 'If there was anyone in there, they're going to have the rest of their life wishing they had complied when I told them to come out!"

The rest of the day, we laid around. That evening, we cooked. The sun had gone down and Sergeant Hicks was sitting with the other Sergeants, Lieutenants and the Captain.

I saw a figure appear from nowhere, not far from Hicks. He walked up to the group and tapped Hicks on the shoulder. Hicks big frame blocked the light from the fire from showing us anything but a silhouette. But when Hicks turned to see who had touched him, a chill ran through me. I dropped my food, grabbed my weapon, and chambered a round as I heard other bolts closing as well. There before

Hicks was a Vietnamese soldier holding his AK-41 weapon out to him.

As Hicks rose and took the rifle, the Vietnamese spoke in broken English, "Please. Food?"

I rushed to the group, along with others and we could see the AK-47 had a thirty round banana clip. The soldier had several bandoleers of ammunition slung over his shoulder and his belt had many grenades hanging from it,

One of the other Sergeants handed the Vietnamese an open can of hot C-rations. The soldier devoured it, using his fingers as a scooping spoon.

Sergeant Hicks stripped the soldier of his grenades, ammunition belts and checked for other weapons.

Next Sergeant Hicks asked the Vietnamese, in English, "Where did you come from?"

The soldier pointed at the ground several meters behind him. We investigated the spot finding a plug of sod beside a small hole. From that position, as heavily armed as the soldier had been, he could have done a lot of damage, killing at least all the Sergeants, and other officers in the group he stood before.

The soldier was given another open can of hot rations as Hicks told me, "Well, Weaver. Why don't you go down there and check that hole out?"

I was starting to think he had it in for me as I asked, "Tonight?"

He replied, "You got something better to do?"

I knew there was no sense arguing. So I answered, "No Sergeant, I'll get my gear."

The hole was very small and I couldn't enter it on my own. I asked, "I need some help. Could a couple of you grab my feet and stuff me in this hole?"

John and Cole came over as I slipped my arms and head into the hole. They each grabbed a leg and shoved forward. I soon had my upper body slipped into the hole only to find my hips being tried to be painfully forced in and failing. No matter how hard they tried, I couldn't be shoved any deeper into the hole.

John and Cole were now really hurting my legs trying to force me into it. Apparently, they couldn't hear me yelling for them to stop, or they were ignoring me.

Soon they stopped on their own and started trying to pull me out. It was to no avail though. It just hurt my legs more. I couldn't take much more of this as fear started sweeping over me. My only hold onto my sanity was my flashlight lighting the hole ahead of me.

After a while, there was no doubt. I was stuck fast and I thought they had given up when they released my legs. That is until I felt the ground shaking. I wasn't looking forward to what I knew was coming next.

Something was tied around my ankles and I could visualize the other end being tied to the APC.

The APC lunged forward, popping me from the hole like a cork from a champagne bottle.

I laid there thinking my ankles were broken. After the rope was removed from my ankles, I balled up and rubbed my ankles, trying to get the pain to stop.

I almost had the circulation back in them when Sergeant Hicks came up and I told him, "I can't make it in that one, Serg."

Sergeant Hicks told Cole, "Drop a grenade in it. The old man said he was alone and the hole doesn't go anywhere. He just got hungry and wanted to give up."

Don dragged me away from the hole as Cole dropped a grenade into it.

The next morning my ankles were fine. As we cooked with C-4, a young soldier came over to me. I assumed he was from the infantry unit. He asked, "How are you guys able to cook your C-rations? I haven't had a hot meal in a week. Would you mind showing me how to do it?"

I answered, "Glad to. Just take some of this..." I pinched him off a little C-4, handed it to him and continued, "Lay it on the ground, light it and cook away."

He took it saying, "Thank you." Turned and rushed off.

About then Sergeant Hicks came over and announced, "Weaver. Get your gear. I've got a big job for you. Of course, for this one, if you don't want to go, I'll understand."

I declared, "You know I'll go, no matter what it is." Hicks informed me, "We have a thousand-pound bomb that didn't go off when dropped the other night. It needs to be blown up."

"I'll go," I responded, laying my can of chicken soup aside. I figured on reheating it when I got back.

After getting instructions on how to find it, I was off across the field to the timberline on the other side. I was out about fifty meters when I heard a little explosion back where I'd come from and a cold chill filled me. By its sound, I was sure that boy had cooked his rations and then probably stepped on the C-4 to put it out. I swore, but continued on to my destination, hoping I was wrong.

I found the short fat bomb easily enough. I placed my C-4 charge on its nose and got ready to set it off. Then I realized, I wanted to sit on it like a horse, just for the hell of it, to be able to later say that I had. If it went off prematurely, it wouldn't matter if I was sitting on top of it or fifty feet away running like hell. That's where I would be blown to. So I straddled it like a horse. I sat there for a moment, satisfying myself before getting off and light the fuse.

I hadn't wanted to run, so I gave myself plenty of fuse and then I headed back across the field.

There was a lot of movement when I arrived. I asked a guy passing, "Hey buddy, while ago there was a little explosion. Could you tell me what caused it?"

My worst fear came alive as he told me, "One of the new guys was cooking with some C-4. He tried to put it out by stomping on it and well..." He shrugged, not finishing his story. He didn't have to as we both knew and we carried on in the direction we had been traveling with me wondering if the boy was even alive now.

I saw medics working on someone and figured it was the boy. I walked that way and yelled once figuring it was almost time, "BIG FIRE IN THE HOLE!"

One medic was between me and the boy's upper body. I could see that the soldier had lost one leg below the knee. The other leg was badly mangled and I hated myself for not instructing him more on the use of C-4.

The medic on the other side of the boy was working on the mangled leg. He looked at me asking, "You need anything?"

I shook my head. "Will he be okay?" I asked.

The medic replied, "He'll live. But he'll lose the rest of the one leg and possibly this one, too. It's busted up pretty good."

All I got out was, "Take care of him, Doc." He nodded as I turned and walked away, wishing I could trade places with the boy. It was all my fault it had happened.

I hadn't walked but a few more feet when my explosion went off. It shook the ground tremendously. I looked back and saw a huge thick cloud rising above the treetops. I stood there watching the cloud spread out and wished it had gone off with me sitting on it.

I couldn't eat my breakfast, so I dumped it. A couple minutes later word came down to load up. We were moving out. So we did.

At the edge of a large number of rice paddies, at least a mile across and half that wide, the Captain had the infantry sit this one out. The tanks and APC's were in line with the engineers aboard them. The engines roared to life and when the order was given, all vehicles raced across the rice paddies with all of the 'sixties' and 'fifties' opening fire out in front of us.

We came to the first dike above water level and all weapons and vehicles stopped turning off their engines. The Captain had the engineers dismounted and checked the dike out. We did and found everything safe. Remounting, the whole process was repeated across the field to the next dike.

After several dikes, we came to one that I had a bad feeling about. I told Hicks about it because I'd been told he believed in such things. I was about to find out if it was true that Hicks never had a man go against his feelings. He told me, "Give me your weapon and get behind this 'fifty! I'll check it out." And I did.

I watched Hicks walk over to the area I would have gone. He was about halfway over the dike when suddenly Hicks stopped in mid-stride. He quickly turned at the waist, looking behind him as something jumped up into the air from where his left foot had just left. At head-level something turned into a white cloud of smoke covering an area several feet wide, including Hicks' head.

As with everyone else, I knew it had been a Bouncing Betty! But this one had been in the ground so long, it was now a dud. For if it had worked properly, as it jumped into the air six to eight feet, it would have exploded, killing everyone in a fifteen-meter radius.

Sergeant Hicks turned pale! His eyes glossed over and He looked like a statue, twisted at the waist. I started to jump off the APC, but Don and Cole were already to him. So I stayed behind the fifty as they led Hicks to the back of the APC.

The driver lowered the back of the track which was a ramp as well and Hicks was ushered inside.

He wasn't physically hurt, just in deep shock. Once again, I was the cause of someone being disabled.

The APC continued until we were at the timberline on the other side. I stayed behind the 'fifty, operating it upon the Sergeants orders.

We stopped at the timberline, waiting for the infantry to come across what we had covered.

We all got down, stretching our legs. Hicks came out of the APC, appearing fine. His eyes were clear and nothing more was ever said about the incident.

A guy from one of the other APC's came over carrying a six-pack of beer. He offered us a cold one. I took one and found he was right. They were cold, like they'd been just taken off ice. John took his and headed for the shade under a tree, while the rest of us sipped on ours where we were.

After the infantry rested a while, the Captain called out from the top of his tank, "LOAD UP!"

Cole called to John, "Okay John, come on." But John didn't move. He just waved Cole off.

Cole and I walked over to John. "Come on..." Cole started. John interrupted him softly, "I can't. I'm sitting on a mine and don't dare move!"

I started to run, but caught myself. After a heart-beat, I told John, "I'll get help." Then I left Cole there and headed first to stop the Captain from moving the column out.

I was thankful the tank's engine hadn't started yet as I told the Captain, "Sir! One of the men sat on a mine! It hasn't gone off. But we have to get him off it."

The Captain called down, "Can you do it?"

"We can Sir, if given enough time."

"Take all you need. Just get that man off it and let me know when you're finished!"

"Yes, Sir!" I said, turning and headed back finding Don had joined Cole with a piece of cardboard and a steel plate.

I watched as Don and Cole seemed to know what they were doing. Cole dug a hole beside John's ass about a foot across and about six inches deep. Working in the hole, Cole slowly brushed dirt away, working his hand under John. Soon, I could see the green color of the mine and Cole announced, "It's a bouncing Betty, all right!"

Cole had now slipped his hand under John, commented after a few seconds, "Okay Don, get the cardboard under him!"

Don carefully slid the cardboard between Cole's hand and John's ass. Once finished, Don then slowly shoved the steel plate over the cardboard and under John, as well.

As Don held the plate down, Cole exclaimed, "Move out, John!" John didn't need to be told twice as he bounced up, running.

Don told me, "You'd better back off as well." And I did.

Now came the hard part. Cole placed his hand beside Don's on the plate, shoving down. Don removed his hand and told Cole, "Good luck." Then he moved off to where I stood and we watched Cole slowly work his hand out from under the cardboard and steel plate, still shoving down constantly on the plate.

Once his hand was out, Cole took a deep breath. Then he rose and took his hand from the plate. He ran, but nothing happened. So it all had worked and everyone was safe.

As Cole joined us, I told him, "Good job." Then looking at Don I added, "You too." And Don just nodded as we got on top of our ride as two infantrymen passed us taking a rope and grappling hook over to pull the plate off the mine.

I called to the Captain, "All finished, Sir." And he waved his response back.

The plate was pulled from a safe distance and the mine did as was expected. It jumped eight feet into the air and exploded. With everyone now aboard, the column moved out.

We hadn't traveled far before we found ourselves moving through a very tall sugar cane field.

We stopped just before exiting the other side. Then word was passed down the line that we would be spending the night here even though it was early.

The sun was still hot out, so I walked out into the open about ten feet or so from the sugar cane. I set my pack on the sand. I slipped off my flak jacket and dropped it over my pack. Then I rested my rifle against this, so it wouldn't fall onto the sand. Then I sat down and leaned my back against my pack opening my shirt and was enjoying being cooler this way.

A shot rang out close. I opened my eyes as another shot followed and I saw men running for cover. I just turned around behind my pack coming up on one knee and the other foot. In no time, I had my weapon up and ready as I scanned for a target.

Someone screamed off to my right and looking, I saw a guy laying on the ground holding his midsection, screaming. I wanted to rush to him, but with bullets whistling in the air, I knew I'd never make it.

No one was responding to the guy's screaming. I yelled, "MEDIC, MEDIC!"

I went to looking for a target. Then about ten feet in front of me, something hit the sand and exploded, throwing sand all over me. I knew instantly it had been a 79 grenade. It made me wonder why I was still alive considering I was well inside the five-meter killing radius of them.

Suddenly, I had another revelation, I remembered having over twenty bricks of C-4 in my pack. If any tracer round that found its way through my pack, all that would be left of me would be a big depression in the sand.

I held my rifle in one hand, while slipping my other through the armhole of my flak jacket and then the straps of my backpack. All in one motion, I rose and ran as fast as I could toward the close-by sugar cane, diving into them when close enough, rolling when I hit the ground.

I pulled my arm out of my pack and jacket as I rolled. I came up on one knee and the other foot flat on the ground as I brought my rifle up to the ready.

I saw Don with Sergeant Hicks and the Captain, working the radio for them. I was close enough that when the Captain looked at the APC about thirty meters out in the opening, I heard him say, "That beehive should clear them out." I looked on top of the track seeing for the first time a 105 Howitzer mounted on top and what was being loaded into its breach. I assumed to be the Beehive. I knew that it contained six thousand barbed darts and would do the job all right.

About then, Don quickly announced, "Captain! It just came through, that's C-company on the other side of those trees! They think we're the enemy and we're doing the same about them!"

At that, the Captain jumped up waving his arms yelling, "APC FOUR, DON'T FIRE THAT TREELINE! CEASE FIRE! CEASE FIRE!"

The guy behind the 105 was ready to pull the cord to set off the round. When he heard the Captain, he quickly opened the breach, ejecting the round as word was sent out to cease fire.

When the Captain called out, "ALL CLEAR." Movement started.

We had two dead, three wounded, and a medevac chopper on its way to pick them up.

It was getting late and as the sun was about to set, all that remained was to eat and then crawl into our sleeping bags beside the vehicle. I announced in passing, "Get your tails undercover, there may be a secondary explosion when the Bunker goes off."

They jumped up as I continued on not looking back to see what they did or where they went.

I got behind the largest tree around and from behind it, I looked back, in the direction from which I had come. The APC crew had run into the back of their vehicle leaving the back ramp down. But the guy on the dune was walking down it, towards me, like he was on a Sunday stroll.

I was hoping there wasn't a bomb besides mine in that Bunker or this guy was in big trouble, possibly dead. Mine would only make that nice clean uniform of his dirty.

My charge went off and there was a secondary explosion! It rocked the area even more than I expected. The percussion blasted the top off the dune. It hit the guy walking so hard, it picked him up and sent him flying through the air, parallel to the ground.

It flipped him end over end and he finally made contact with the ground, hitting it very hard!

I ducked behind the tree as dust, sand, and other materials flew past my tree.

When everything settled down, I came out from behind the tree to see if everyone was okay.

The first thing I saw was the guy from the dune. He was slowly stirring, so I knew he was at least alive.

The guys in the APC came out of it, holding their ears for the night.

At 1730 hours, Sergeant Hicks walked up to me and said, "Weaver. Before it gets completely dark, I've got a Bunker needing to be blown up. You up to it?"

I picked up my pack and answered, "I'm always up for that."

He led the way to the top of a sand dune, pointing to an old type Bunker, half below ground level and Sergeant Hicks explained, "I know you've been told before, but I'm stressing it, sometimes the enemy plants mines in abandoned Bunkers hoping we'll go in them, step on them and blowing us up. So probe it out." I nodded answering, with a smile, "I fully plan to."

I left the Sergeant and at the entrance to the Bunker, I laid my weapon and pack down, then I took out my probing knife and started working my way inside, gently shoving my wooden knife into the ground at an angle feeling for any obstacle buried under it. About midway inside, where I planned to set my charge. I left my knife in the ground to show where I stopped and went to retrieve a forty pound charge of explosives.

Returning, I placed it where I wanted, lit the fuse, giving myself about ten minutes, I exited the Bunker, grabbed my pack and rifle, yelling our as loud as I could, "FIRE IN THE HOLE! FIRE IN THE HOLE!" And I headed for the sand dune.

A man was standing on top of the dune with his hands on his hips. He was looking the terrain over as I ran past him, not even looking at his rank, not caring. I shouted at him not stopping my stride, "Get your ass under cover!" And I proceeded on down the other side of the dune. As I approached the bottom of it, I heard the guy I had just passed calling after me, "Come back here, soldier!" But I just ignored him and continued on toward the timber line. I came to an APC where its crew was relaxing on their Army cots, and I guessed they had ignored my call, so I announced in passing, "Get your ass's under cover, they may be a secondary explosion when mine goes off in the Bunker over the dune." They jumped up as I continued on not looking back to see what they did or where they went. I got behind the largest tree around and from behind it, I looked back in the direction from which I had come. The APC crew had run into the back of their vehicle leaving the back ramp down, which was away from the blast if it came. But the guy on the dune was walking down it, towards me, like he was in a Sunday stroll. I was hoping there wasn't a bomb besides mine in that Bunker or this guy was in big trouble, possibly dead. Mine would only make that nice clean uniform of his dirty. My charge went off and there was a big secondary explosion! It rocked the area even more than I expected. The percussion blasted the top of the dune off. It hit the guy walking down it so hard, it picked him up, sending him flying through the air, parallel to the ground, flipping him head over heels and hitting the ground very hard. I ducked behind the tree as dust, sand and other material flew past my tree. When every-thing settled down, I came out from behind the tree to see if everyone was okay. As I approached the APC, the guys inside were just exiting it. Passing on by, I could see its 'fifty caliber and both 'sixties had been torn off their mounts. But I couldn't see where they were now. The cots left beside the vehicle were broken and covered with dirt, sand and small pieces of wood.

The guy from the dune was on his feet brushing himself off and that is when I saw the Silver Star on his shoulders. I knew I was in trouble, but I stood my ground. As my father would have said at a time like this, "He can kill you son, but he can't eat you. That's against the food law."

As he came up to me, l could see he was madder than hell, but I figured it was his own damn fault.

He stopped about a foot from me, pointing on the star on his shoulder. He angrily asked me, "You know what this is, soldier? You don't run past me, talking to me like you did and you're to give a clearer warning before setting off any explosions."

I stood there not knowing what to say, I had called out "Fire in the Hole." Maybe I didn't call it out as many times as I should have, but it was loud enough for everyone else.

Suddenly Sergeant Hicks pushed between us, facing the General, speaking more harshly than the General had. "He did, Sir! Now, I'd advise, with all due respect, Sir, you get your ass on that chopper before I blow it away! These men are who will get you and your little star home."

The General quickly spun hurrying to his chopper and a few minutes later he was airborne. Then Sergeant Hicks turned to me and spoke a little calmer. "Next time, salute the bastard so a sniper can shoot him in his shiny star." Then he walked away.

It was completely dark when I found Don and we cooked a meal while I told him what had happened. We laughed about the General and his reaction to the Sergeant's words. A little later I drifted off to sleep.

I awoke to a lot of movement and knew if I didn't hurry, I'd be busy until lunch without eating. I got up and put my things together for traveling. Then I fixed myself some breakfast.

Today I felt like walking, so I told Sergeant Hicks and he replied "I'll join you. It'll do some good." So placing our packs on the back of the APC, we followed in its tracks, finding it hard sometimes to keep up. This mission had sounded simple when we left base, but it was turning into something from Hell, I wasn't even grasping half of it yet.

When everything seemed to be moving smoothly, I asked Hicks, "What happened yesterday, sarge?"

Sergeant Hicks explained, "A few gooks got between us and Charlie Company. They took a few shots at both sides before ducking out and leaving us to shoot it out between ourselves. "But it could have been more disastrous than it was. Those things happen."

I didn't respond. I just went into deep thought as we entered the woods and started up the side of a mountain.

The higher we went, the harder the climb got and it was even harder on the APC's that had to weave through the trees.

I was having to use trees to help myself along, grabbing one pulling myself to it, then another to assist my ascent up the mountain. It just got harder and harder.

I wondered how the APC's were able to make it up this slope. They must have some mountain goat in them to do that. Right now, l wished my ass was on an APC.

As l reached for another tree, suddenly an alarm went off in my head. I froze, moving just my eyes to scan for the danger my senses were alerting me about. I had learned to trust them way back when hunting at home.

I couldn't find any danger. I was thinking that maybe my senses were on the blink today and started to move my hand the few inches to the fork of the next tree to pull myself further up. However, that was when I saw movement I had missed before.

I jerked my hand away from the tree, because in the fork of the tree was the head of a Bamboo Viper. The snake's head was swaying back and forth, ready to strike at my hand.

I had been just inches from certain death. The Bamboo Viper can grow up to about an inch in diameter and up to about eighteen inches long. Their camouflage was natural, being the same color green as the leaves of the trees. That's why so many people get bit and die three seconds later.

A chill went down my spine thinking about this. So I gave the tree a wide birth. I went on up the mountain until I found Sergeant Hicks.

After telling him what had happened, he said, "Let's go find this unwanted guest before someone else decides to grab onto that same tree." I carefully led the way.

It took a while, but we finally found it and the snake's head was still swaying back and forth, looking for something to strike.

Sergeant Hicks pulled out his pistol, took the safety off and placed the end of the barrel inches from the snake's head. Hicks then moved the pistol closer to the snake as its head backed away. I knew Sergeant Hicks was playing with danger, because the snake had the ability to strike along the side of the pistol to bite his hand.

He pulled the trigger and dust was raised from the fork of the tree as the snake disappeared. We moved closer and found the snake's headless body twisting on the ground. There we saw its mate trying to escape. Hicks' pistol roared again, eliminating the problem and we headed back up the mountain.

As we climbed, we could no longer hear the engines of the APC's or tanks. I asked Hicks, "You think we lost the others."

"I doubt it. We'll probably find them just a bit further up ahead."

Sure enough, about sixty meters further, we came to five of the APC's and one tank in line facing up the mountain. Their engines were off and I could see all the men sitting along the edge of a cliff to our right. They were all looking down over a small grassy valley about fifty meters square, lined all the way around by trees.

I found Don, sitting with the Captain. I joined them and told them about the snakes. Don whistled softly. I offered, "How about I take over the radio. You've been lugging it for a while now. I'll give you a break."

Don answered as he turned so I could help him shed it, "Thanks. I could use the break. We're in contact with our company. All you have to remember is that you're 'Raven' and they're 'Blackbird.' Got it? "I nodded and he helped me put the radio on my back.

We sat talking softly and about half an hour later, the Captain commented, "Will you look at that!"

Everyone looked to where he was pointing. There, moving across the valley floor about a hundred meters below us, we could see about fifty Vietnamese soldiers in full uniform. They were carrying weapons and walking across the valley like no one else was around. Sergeant Hicks exclaimed, "Damn! Hard-core regulars!"

This was my first time seeing a sight like this and I didn't have long to wait before the Captain told me, "Call it in and get us permission to fire."

"Yes, Sir," I answered. I keyed the mike and spoke into it, "Raven calling Blackbird. Come in Blackbird. Over."

Not getting a reply, I keyed the mike repeating myself.

This time an answer came back, "Raven, this is Blackbird. Over."

I relayed everything and was told, "Hold Raven. Over." I told the Captain that they'd put me on hold.

Seeing the Vietnamese almost three-quarters of the way across the field, he angrily said, "They don't know what they're doing back there! They'd have to call it in if they wanted to wipe their asses! "Bureaucracy!" Why won't they just let us fight this war? Christ, by the time they get their fingers out of their asses, we'll have lost it!"

As the Vietnamese entered the timber, the voice on the radio said, "Raven, this is Blackbird. Come in Raven. Over."

I told the Captain as Blackbird repeated himself, "They're on the line now, Captain." He didn't move nor reply, so I keyed the mike answering, "This is Raven, go ahead Blackbird. Over."

Blackbird replied, "You have permission to fire. Report back when finished. Over."

I told the Captain, who exclaimed, raising his voice, "What do those assholes want us to shoot at?"

I asked him, "You want me to ask them, Sir?" He nodded. I keyed the mike and asked after making contact, "The Captain would like to know who you assholes want us to shoot at? You took so long they're gone now. You got any ideas?"

I didn't have to say "over" this time. Getting no immediate reply, I didn't know if this was because of my language or if they were trying to come up with an answer to cover up their mistake.

I didn't have long to wait before a voice on the radio said, "Raven, your orders are to send a patrol out and capture as many as possible. Do you understand your orders, Raven? Over."

I relayed the order to the Captain who swore fiercely before

170

telling me, "I wish they'd go down there and capture them their own damned selves. But tell them, 'Understood.'

I did as the Captain said and he left.

About an hour later, a lot of shooting erupted. It didn't last very long and we knew the patrol had caught up with the Vietnamese troops.

When the Captain did return, he sat down exhausted, informing me, "Contact Blackbird and tell them, 'mission accomplished.' We have thirty prisoners, but we sustained eight dead and six wounded! Not a good exchange, if you ask me!"

Everyone stayed silent while I contacted Blackbird and reported. Blackbird told me medevac choppers were on their way and would meet us on top of the mountain. I relayed this to the Captain and then we moved out.

The climb up the mountain took about forty-five minutes, but it was uneventful.

Helicopters were everywhere, waiting for us when we arrived on top and ten minutes later, they left carrying the prisoners, wounded and dead.

It was almost 1800 hours and I figured we were going to stay there for the night. I was wrong. We moved out immediately and an hour later, we were off the mountain heading across semi-flat land in the dark. Word finally came that we would move for one more hour and then stop for the night.

We hadn't moved for more than fifty feet when green tracers started streaking across the area from automatic weapons.

We hit the ground, not knowing from where the shots were coming. But the tracers being green told us it wasn't friendly fire! It was definitely VC.

As several soldiers returned fire, Sergeant Hicks shouted to me, "Call for flare ships, Weaver. Now!" And he started shooting, too.

I keyed the mike and shouted over the shooting, "Blackbird, this is Raven! Come in Blackbird! Over,"

There wasn't any delay this time, "Go ahead Raven. This is Blackbird, What's your problem? Over."

I yelled, "We're under fire and need flare ships! Now! Over." I gave them our coordinates and the waiting began as the shooting got intense.

We heard the choppers and knew it was the flare ships. When the sound of the first flare popped, leaving its container, it lit up the area nicely. It was followed by many others and soon the whole area was lit up brightly.

The only scary part of the flares were the large metal containers. They measured maybe four inches in diameter and were approximately two and a half feet long. They'd come down whistling to the ground, hitting with a loud impact after the flare had popped free. I also knew that nobody would survive if they were hit by one.

The flare ships continued circling, lighting up the area while the shots continued. But it wasn't as fierce as before.

About half an hour later, everything got quiet. The only noise came from the choppers and its flares popping from their canisters. Sergeant Hicks called over to me, "Okay, Weaver. Tell 'em thanks and if we need more, we'll call again." So I contacted Blackbird and relayed the message.

We stayed put, taking turns sleeping, because there were no other activities going on.

Dawn broke and movement started. Slowly at first, I got up

and walked out the stiffness in my body. Then someone yelled, "OVER HERE!"

We joined the caller and found one of the snipers that had kept us pinned down most of the night.

From the sniper's waist down, he was still in his hideaway hole. From his waist up, he laid flat on the ground with his arms out in front of him, still grasping his AK-47. One of the flare canisters had come down hitting him just as he was about to squeeze off more rounds at us. It had drilled him in the back of the head and there wasn't much left of it now.

It was appearing that he shot at us from one place, then moved underground, only to come up someplace else. Then he'd shoot and do it all over again. It only took a few shots now and then to keep us pinned down all night. If there were others with this guy, they were gone now.

Someone said, "Score one for the flare ship." And a roar of laughter erupted as everyone left to get ready to move out.

The sky was completely clouded over this morning and I could feel rain in the air. I got my rain gear out and had no sooner gotten them on, when the sky opened up like nothing I'd ever experienced before.

I cooked some C-rations and ate as best I could. I was thinking I'd ride inside the APC today, but it wasn't to be. Thirty minutes later, we got word to move out. Sergeant Hicks instructing me, "Stick with me today, Weaver." So I did and it rained heavily all day. I was thankful Cole had taken over the radio and I didn't have to carry it in the rain.

We had traveled only a few hours when all hell broke loose. Green tracers streaked through the air from more directions than I wanted to take time to count. It was like we had walked into a hornets nest. However, rather than run as if bees were after us, everyone hit the ground, splashing into the rice paddies filled with about eight inches of water.

Holding my rifle up out of the water as best I could, I flipped the safety off and pointing it in front of me. I squeezed off a whole clip.

I rolled onto my side, dropped the empty clip, fished out a full one and put it in my rifle. I let the bolt slam home, then I emptied it into the surrounding brush in front of me as enemy bullets whizzed past my head.

Soon the rain let up, almost stopping, but the shooting continued. I was down to my last few clips, so I gathered my empties putting them into my wet and soaked pockets.

Staying low, I made my way to the inside of an APC and commenced to filling my empty clips.

Scrounging around, I found some extra clips and added them to my own. Seeing as I was wet to the skin, I took a little time to remove the rain gear, I put them in my pack, giving myself some freedom of movement. Then I eased out of the APC, my arms loaded with bandoleers and my pockets full of grenades.

Outside, I tried to decide which way to go. The shooting had stopped and I couldn't see any movement. I saw Hicks just a few meters away, so I crouched low and scurried over to him without drawing fire.

Dropping to the ground beside him. "What now?" I asked him.

Sergeant Hicks announced, "We're in the soup this time. It's about as bad as it gets. We're waiting for word on what to do."

I interrupted him, "Besides the obvious, what is our situation?"

"Remember, we were told two divisions were out here?" I nodded and he went on, "Well, they were partly right. They just told me that the two divisions have dug in. The reason why it's been so easy pushing them back, they were really drawing us in. That is until now, for it seems we have walked over a division waiting for us to pass. Now they have popped up and are between us and the mainland, preventing any retreat off this peninsula. To make things worse, we have the ocean on both sides of us, full of Sam Pans (small flat-bottom Vietnamese boats) waiting for us."

I interjected arrogantly, "All we need is the covered wagons, huh?" And Hicks pointed at the APC's not commenting. But then, he didn't have to, those were our covered wagons.

Now he instructed, "Find a place and dig in. It's going to get rough any moment. Can you spare any of them bandoleers?"

"Sure Sarge," I said and dropped them all beside him as well as emptied my pockets.

Then I made my way back to the APC still without drawing fire.

Inside, I opened several cans, filling my arms with as many bandoleers as I could carry and my pockets full of grenades, then eased back out taking my entrenching tool from my pack.

I went in the opposite direction of Hicks and quickly dug a furrow to lay in, having found a place out of the rice paddy.

It still filled with water no matter how much I bailed it out with my helmet liner. So after a while, I gave up and crawled in.

I was wet, muddy, and tired. If only I could have gotten a

shower and dry clothes, it would have made all the difference in the world. But I laid there quietly and looked for a target.

"Hi, Ward." A low voice said from behind me and I quickly looked around to find it was John.

I said, "Hi, yourself. What're you doing here?"

He laid down beside me, taking off his pack, then he answered, "I thought you needed company. You mind?"

I handed him my shovel responding, "Use it."

John, took it, quickly making a trench for himself and had it just about as he needed it when the shooting started again.

Green and red tracers crisscrossed the air from every direction. I flipped off the safety never looking at John, but instead, was trying to find a target. I told him, "Keep digging! I'll cover you!" And then I fired, emptying a clip into the foliage in front of us.

I snapped out the empty clip, replaced it with a full one, then quickly glanced to see how John was doing. He was in his furrow pulling his pack in front of him. I emptied another clip while he finished.

Bullets smashed into the ground all around us and I dropped my head, feeling sick as I heard another bullet whizzing past us. I remembered my night fire training in Missouri. It wasn't anything like this. Whoever was keeping John's and my head down seemed to be zeroing in on our position. I needed to know where he was and I figured it'd better be soon.

I raised my head slowly, my rifle too, and squeezed off a few rounds in the direction I thought the target was hiding. Then I ducked down after seeing the muzzle flash of my target, who was situated a little to the right from where I had been firing.

176

Sweat or rain, I wasn't sure which, ran down my face. But surprisingly, I was feeling better now, seemingly getting my fear under control.

The shooting didn't let up. But I stopped long enough to fill empty clips.

I was filling the last one when I heard someone yell, "HERE THEY COME!"

I took up my rifle quickly looking toward the foliage and the sight was blood stopping. Something only from the movies could describe it accurately. Words were inadequate as wave after wave of Vietnamese were emerging from the wood. There were literally hundreds of them, maybe even thousands.

The sound of shooting got more intense as red and green tracers filled the air even more than before.

Almost deafened by the sound of the tanks firing their ninety-millimeter rounds, plus grenades exploding. I could just hear the yelling and screaming of pain over it all. Adrenaline was pumping as I emptied one clip after another, paying no attention to the figures that kept falling.

It seemed like for every Vietnamese that went down, three more took his place. They came like an unstoppable wave as men screamed from pain. Others were yelling for medics and I did my best to close my ears to it as I emptied more clips. But I found it hard to block it all out.

I didn't have time to hate as the Vietnamese kept coming. It was like there was no end to them. I was just working automatically now.

I ran out of full clips and frantically looked for one that might have gotten missed with ammunition still it. But there wasn't any! So leaving my weapon on the ground, I grabbed a grenade and pulled the pin. I let the handle go, counted to three and threw it. I grabbed another repeating the actions, then used another and another.

I was oblivious to the other explosions and soon I was throwing them without even counting. I was just pulling pins and throwing.

Suddenly I heard John yell, "PUFF'S HERE!"

Holding the handle down on the grenade I'd just pulled the pin from, I stayed laying down and looked up to see Puff. Puff was a cargo plane with the back window on each side taken out. An electric-operates mini-Gatling Gun was mounted at these two windows, each able to fire six-thousand rounds a minute.

I saw it open up on the timberline, sounding like a fog horn going off in short fifteen-second intervals. A feeling of peace went through me, knowing that whatever happened to us, at least a whole lot of them were going with us!

Puff was not only beautiful, but it sounded fantastic. The firing lasted for the full minute of ammunition that it carried.

As the plane left, John called out, "'IT'S OVER! They broke and are running!" I hadn't realized the shooting had stopped until that moment.

Looking out over the killing zone, except for the bodies lying everywhere, the rest had vanished. I checked myself, replacing the pin in the grenade. I then took a second to relax all my muscles, which was a mistake because I started shaking uncontrollably.

John laid a hand on my shoulder saying, "We've got to get ready, buddy."

I got control of myself, knowing he was right and started scanning for movement as I worked to reload my clips and John went for more ammunition.

I was filling a clip when I saw movement in the trees. I dropped the clip, grabbed my weapon and emptied a clip into the spot in which I'd seen the movement. There was no return fire, so I laid my rifle down and went back to re-loading more clips.

Feeling better that all my clips were full, as were John's, who had returned from the APC having brought more grenades as well.

Suddenly what I thought was an artillery round went over-head. It sounded like a locomotive going over or possibly going to land in the hole with me. I yelled, "INCOMING!" And dropped as low as possible into my furrow, holding my rifle in one hand, my other against the top of my helmet, shoving down and keeping my mouth open. We'd learned to do that for such explosions.

The explosion wasn't long in coming and it was deafening as it shook the ground violently.

'Damn, what was that?' I thought, having never experienced anything like it in training. I raised my head and yelled over to Sergeant Hicks, "What in the hell was that? No one said anything about them gooks having artillery!"

He shook his head responding, "They're sixteen-inch rounds from The New Jersey. They're giving us support fire. So stay as low as possible." And we did.

The next one sounded and felt even closer. The explosion was even more violent than before and I wished my hole was a deeper one, even if it filled with water.

Shrapnel whistled close overhead. Then someone shouted

what I wasn't expecting, "HERE THEY COME AGAIN!" And looking, there was a huge mass of figures rushing from the trees and the shooting got as fierce as before. It wasn't hard to find a target as I replaced clip after clip into my weapon.

One figure that emerged from the treeline seemed to be running directly at me as I put in a new clip. I never took my eyes off the guy, amazed at the distance he covered in such a short time period.

I aimed, fired, and his body dropped behind a log in such a manner that I wasn't sure if I'd hit him or he had just dropped for cover.

More rounds from the New Jersey came in and though still going off in the timberline, they seemed to fall like rain. Each shell would send shrapnel everywhere. Even our way and I would try to get even lower into my furrow than the last time.

An eternity passed, but the shooting never eased and I wished Puff would return, but he never did.

I reloaded several times, thankful the rain had been merciful and stopped altogether as the sea of men continued to come.

As I replaced another clip, John called out, "Ward, I'm out, you got any extra?"

I looked to see how many bandoleers I had left with ammunition in them and found only one. I told John as I threw him the bandoleer, "I'm down to my last couple clips. I'll go get some more."

When I looked back toward the trees and brush, the figure that had dropped behind the log rose and began rushing me again. Both John and I opened up and in mid-stride, he spun like a top and hit the ground face down, dead this time, I hoped.

The number of figures coming now was sporadic. So I prepared to head for the APC when suddenly another big wave of men burst from the timber and we opened up yet again.

John yelled, "I'm out, I've got to make it to the APC. I'll bring back enough for both of us."

I shouted to him, not looking, "After the next round goes off, go." We heard it coming in and we hugged the ground.

After it went off, I yelled, "GO!" and then I opened up, emptying two clips before glancing to see if he had made it. He was just entering the APC.

I checked and found the only ammo I had left was the full clip I was putting into my rifle right now. I hoped John wouldn't be long as I saved that clip and instead, started pulling the pins from grenades. I began throwing them as fast as I could pick one up and pull the pin.

I saw John exit the APC and I stopped throwing grenades. I picked up my weapon and though the shooting was the same, the only movement I could see, between us and the trees now, were a few on the ground trying to crawl back into the timber-line. Of these I could see, most were covered with blood.

I looked back to see John bent over and coming fast. He looked kind of funny, burdened as he was, both arms loaded with bandoleers.

As John raced towards me, bullets kicked up rice water all around him and I knew someone was trying to stop John from getting to me. So I opened up, giving him as much cover as I could.

I heard another round from the New Jersey coming in. My clip was empty and I ducked, hoping John was doing the same. There was no way he could make it to his furrow next to mine in time.

The explosion went off. It was so deafening and the ground shook so violently, I knew the round hadn't made it to the timberline. Shrapnel whistled so close overhead, I swore I could feel the heat from it.

When it was safe, I jerked my head around to make sure John was okay. Horror filled me. John's body lay at my feet, a piece of shrapnel had literally taken his head off. I looked away, almost vomiting.

I tried to check myself, but I was unable to stop myself from shaking violently as time and sound became non-existent.

A hand grabbed my shoulder and I rolled over to defend myself. My right hand went for my bayonet, leaving my empty rifle where it was laying. I expected a bayonet to be thrust into me at any moment. I was going to try to take the bastard with me!

Time seemed to move in slow motion and I had my knife halfway out when a familiar voice said, "Hold it! It's me! Sergeant Hicks!"

I froze and Sergeant Hicks laid down beside me in John's dug out furrow, keeping his hand on my shoulder. I said, "Sorry. John's..." I couldn't finish.

Sergeant Hicks responded, "Yeah, he's gone, but you're okay, aren't you?"

I replied nodding, "But it should have been me there!"

Hicks told me sternly, "It was his time! Now pull yourself together! We could get hit again at any moment! Maybe this time it will be your time. But until then, at least John brought you what you needed to take as many of them bastards with you as possible."

I nodded, getting ahold of myself, I rose, as did Sarge and we collected the bandoleers and grenades from John's body.

We now set to work, loading clips as fast as we could.

The day wore on and evening came. The fighting had resumed, getting fierce several times. During each lull, I would make the trip to the APC getting more ammunition and grenades. Then I would return to my furrow and luck was with me. We survived the day and into the evening.

During one break in the shooting, Hicks left me for a while. Upon returning, he informed me, "We've got to hold out until morning. Then the APC's will cross the line for home, carrying the wounded and dead. Choppers will then come in and take us out. You got enough ammunition to hold out until morning?"

"I think so." Then he dropped several bandoleers beside me and then left to get more and tell the others the same news he had told me.

The weather decided it had held off long enough and now opened the gates to let the rain come down hard. It was difficult to see very far in any direction. But I started shooting in the general direction the green tracers were originated, when they once again were flying in our direction.

That night was the longest one of my life. Flare ships kept the area lit up like day, Gunships aided us and several times I thought this night could be my last.

But morning did come. I found myself still alive, with only three clips of ammunition left and all the bandoleers empty.

The only good thing was the shooting tapered off to just a shot now and then, mostly off in the distance.

I was more exhausted than I ever remembered being before. I just wanted to close my eyes and let the world do its worst. However, there was more than just my life at stake.

Men moved about and by their size, I knew they were ours. Probably getting into better positions while the shooting had let up. So I rose, heading for the APC for more bandoleers and grenades.

Before entering the vehicle, I saw Don several meters on the other side helping a medic carry a wounded man to a safe place.

I dropped to one knee, brought my weapon up to give them as much cover as the ammunition I had left would allow, if they needed it. But they soon had the guy safely inside one of the APC's.

Don had seen me and after he exited the APC, he made his way to me and said, "How you doing? I've been worried about you."

After telling him I was just fine and had been concerned about him as well. I told him about John. He told me that Hicks had already told him. So I asked, "Did he tell you about the APC's leaving and our being airborne out if we last long enough?"

Don answered, "Yeah, I hope it's soon." Then we crawled inside the APC where we loaded up with ammunition and grenades before taking a moment to just rest and relax. My muscles were cramping like never before.

We were crawling out when Sergeant Hicks appeared. He told us, "I'm glad you two are loaded up. The APC's leave in fifteen minutes." And he entered the APC, to load up as we left for the spot in which I had spent the night. John's body had already been taken away.

Right on time, the APC's, carrying the dead and wounded, as well as the tanks, headed out with all of their automatic weapons firing to clear their path of any possible Vietnamese lying in wait.

Once they were out of sight, Sergeant Hicks told us all, "The choppers are on their way. So let's set the L.Z. (Landing Zone) right here. Spread out and when the choppers come in give that timberline everything you have. Give the choppers all the cover they need. L.Z.'s are being set up in other areas as well."

Ten minutes later, they flew in and we were ready as they appeared over the trees. Before we could fire though, the sky around the choppers was streaking with green tracers. We opened fire and so did the gunners on the choppers.

Six helicopters came in together, looking beautiful. I emptied one clip after another into the timberline, not caring now much ammunition I used. My empties were slipped into my pockets. We all had our packs on and ready to go.

The first wave of eight engineers and infantrymen loaded onto the chopper as the enemy concentrated their fire on the choppers, even though we were pouring everything we could at them.

As the second wave of men headed for our rescuers, one of the chopper's engines sputtered and then the whole helicopter dropped out of the sky like a rock. Everyone knew it had been hit by rifle fire, but thankfully it didn't explode on impact. So many of them did in situations like this.

The pilot and co-pilot bailed out, running from the wreckage as fast as they could, followed by their gunners.

The other choppers were lifting quickly off the ground and another six came in as if nothing had happened to one of their own.

The next wave of men boarded the choppers and Don called out as we continued firing, "We're next Ward! Get ready!" And I was.

I was so thankful, because I was down to my last two clips.

As the six came in, they didn't even stop. They just scooted across the ground and Don and I ran for the closest one to us.

Don made it in before I did. I was the last man in again. I dove in and turned around quickly. I found the place fuller than I expected.

I was barely inside and had to sit with just my ass perched on the edge of the door, my legs hanging outside with nothing to grab hold unto.

The chopper jumped into the air so fast, I felt sure my stomach had been left on the ground. Then the chopper banked drastically and I gasped. I was sitting upright, looking straight ahead and was looking at the ground directly in front of me. I wondered what was holding me in and expected to fall out of the chopper at any second. I'd fall hard on the ground, a very long way down!

Green tracers from the ground whizzed all around us and I expected to be hit by one as well. They were answered by the choppers' gunners firing their 'sixties.

I wasn't feeling very secure until we leveled off well out of danger. Then I realized centrifugal force had kept me in the chopper when it banked so steeply. I felt kind of foolish having not remembered this when panic had its clutches on me. As I relaxed, I suddenly felt guilty about my cowardly actions earlier. When I couldn't control my body's reaction. I sure hoped no one would find out. I wasn't paying attention to the scenery as we flew back to the trucks waiting to take us back to the company compound.

We were quickly deposited on the ground and we loaded up on the trucks as the choppers lifted off again, heading off to another mission.

We headed back to the showers, clean clothes, hot meals and sleep. The trucks moved along Highway One and we rode in silence. My mind was on the men that hadn't made it off the peninsula alive and how many of them died from our own people's carelessness.

The men who came in on the other waves of evacuation ahead of us were waiting at the company loading area when we arrived. So we joined them, waiting for the rest.

It was about twenty minutes later when the last wave showed up. Sergeant Hicks took inventory and found our casualties consisted of Milt Flowers, Jack Hitching, Sam Sutton, and John Smith all dead. Paul Logan and John Moore were wounded, but not seriously.

Sergeant Hicks had gotten a flesh wound in his side while getting on the chopper. He had been with the last taken out. He just had it bandaged up and refused to go to the hospital.

As we started for the Hooch, Sergeant Hicks came up beside me saying, "You did right good out there, Weaver. I had my eye on you. I won't have to worry about you anymore. At first, I'd had my doubts about you. But you learn fast and keep yourself in control. Welcome aboard." And he patted me on the back.

"Thank you, Sarge." but I knew he hadn't forgotten about my losing control the day before. So I figured he was giving me a second chance, knowing I wouldn't let him down next time.

Inside the Hooch, I sat my gear on the floor and we all began cleaning up and replacing what was needed. I had to cut my clothes and boots off because they were so caked with mud that they had dried hard.

After we had everything put away, we headed for the showers. I stood under the spray for a long time, letting it work on the soreness of my shoulders and neck muscles.

After dressing, Don and I headed for the mess hall where I found myself hungrier than I had thought I'd be. The food even tasted better than I remembered.

When we finished, I told Don, "Bring in a crane and a doctor. I need both."

"Why both?"

I chucked before telling him, "The crane's to get me back to the Hooch and the doctors to pump my stomach out. I just ate too much." Don laughed and was joined by the others at the table.

When we got back to the Hooch, we went to bed and I was instantly sound asleep.

The next morning, when I got up, Don was still sleeping. So I went to supply and found Gary reading a magazine. I greeted him with, "Hi Gary. What's new?"

"Nothing much," he answered before pointing at a box at the other end of the counter and continued, "I've got several boxes of new clips in, but I've got no place to put them." He shook his head, lowering his hand.

I suggested, "How about letting me take a few off your hands?

I was a little short this last time and would sure like to have had twice as many as I did."

Gary hesitated, closed his magazine, then said, "I can't. But I've got to go in the back for a while and if some are gone when I come back, I doubt I'll ever know about it until inventory. Maybe not even then." And he went to the back of the building.

I loaded my pockets with clips, then turned to leave calling out, "Thanks Gary, see you later."

Gary inquired, "Thanks for what?"

"The conversation." He waved over his shoulder as I exited the building.

I was just passing the corner of the supply building when Gary's voice stopped me, "Hey, Weaver! I forgot to give you a letter that was left for you a few days ago."

I took the envelope, thanked him and finished going to the Hooch. I laid the envelope aside while I cleaned the new clips. Then I filled each with eighteen rounds before putting them in my pack.

Don was still asleep, so I took the envelope Gary gave me and opened it. I found only a strip of negative inside. I held them up to the light and all four negatives were of Joe, the Vietnamese that had gotten shot to hell in front of the Bunker. The guy that almost got me court-martialed. I quickly hid the film in my footlocker.

About 1100 hours, Don woke and I told him, "I was going to toe-tag you as dead. Hurry up and we'll go get some lunch."

Smiling, Don rose getting dressed and we were off to the mess hall.

The rest of the day we just laid around, resting and after supper we got our gear and headed out to see a movie. Tonight, it was a World War II movie.

Right in the middle of a very intense battle scene, everyone was totally wrapped up in it, someone behind us fired his weapon.

I bent over, grabbing my gear and stood. I scanned the area and found I was suddenly alone. Not a soul was in sight, nor could I see any movement. I wondered where the eleven or so people were, that seconds ago had been sitting around me, watching the show.

Not moving during this interval query, I also realized that the shot had probably come from one of the guys that had gotten too involved in the movie. The guy had shot the screen to help kill the Japanese. I sat back down, placed my gear back on the ground and continued watching the show, as if nothing had happened.

It wasn't long before I sensed movement around me, but I didn't take my eyes off the screen. I didn't want anyone to think the shot had bothered me.

When a hand touched my shoulder, I looked up and saw it was Don. I asked him casually, "Did you bring back any popcorn from the snack bar?"

I kept a straight face as he inquired, "What stopped you?"

I played it off, "You mean the shot? Oh, I knew all along it was an accident. I just thought you went to get some..."

Don interrupted me, "Bullshit! I saw you jump up."

So I confessed, explaining what happened and finished with, "I can't see how everyone moved so fast?"

Don laughed before responding, "After these past eleven days you can still ask that?"

I asked him very seriously now, looking at him, "Do you ever get so scared out there that you want to run?"

Don studied my face for a second before replying, "All the time. Especially when being shot at. Didn't you, when we were under attack out there?"

I explained what happened and about how Hicks had calmed me down at one point. I had to tell someone and Don was the only person I trusted. We were like brothers and I even expressed my thoughts of feeling like a coward since then.

Don was deep in thought and at that moment the movie ended.

We gathered up our things and then headed for the Hooch. Don told me as we walked, "Welcome to the human race."

I stopped and puzzled, saying, "HUH?"

Don stopped and facing me said, "I was starting to wonder about you and your love for blowing up things. You've volunteered for more missions in the past eleven days while we were out, than me or anyone else here has been on in all the months we've been here. But that's okay, as long as you stay scared!"

"Thanks, Don. You are a good friend." And we walked on.

The next day started off good. Everyone was just relaxing and waiting for orders to go out again. The rain raged on with fury and for four days, we only left the Hooch to eat. Paul and John came back from the hospital. Replacements arrived with them. But only one was assigned to our squad. His name was Jerry Gunther and to me, he looked like a book worm type, but likable.

The rain stopped sometime during the fifth night and the next day, the sun came out hot and the humidity was very high. It was almost like trying to breathe water into our lungs.

Sergeant Baker, whom I'd not seen since Bang Song bridge incident, came in asking, "I need volunteers for a mine sweeping detail. We have any in here?"

I didn't like any part of mine detecting, so I said, "Sorry Sergeant, I never was any good at telling the difference in those beeps. So I wouldn't be any use to you," And I hoped my lie wouldn't be detected.

Cole came up with basically the same story. I was sure Sergeant Baker knew we were both lying, but he had asked for volunteers.

Paul came forward, so did the new guy, Jerry. Sergeant Baker told Jerry, "Gunther, you just came in, so you'd better sit this one out. Thanks for the offer anyway. I need experienced people on this one. "

After Paul left with Baker, I asked Don, "Got any money?"

He dug into his pocket and after counting what he had, Don said, "Eight dollars and forty cents. But I need five of it to mail a package tomorrow and buy a few things I need from the P.X."

I took the three dollars and forty cents, added it to my own, then asked Jerry, "You want to contribute and I'll go get the beer?"

Jerry handed me five dollars asking, "Is that good enough?"

"Great," I replied heading for the club where I bought four cases of beer, which was all I could carry.

Back in the Hooch, we began drinking. Jerry didn't like the

taste of the Ballantine, until we told him there wasn't any other kind around. Then he started drinking beer for beer with the rest of us.

I woke the next morning with my head throbbing, feeling like it was about to burst open. I just laid there with my eyes closed, hoping it would go away and afraid that it wouldn't.

A hand shook me and I said, "It'd better be good."

Don's voice declared as if talking to a little kid, "Did we drink too much last night?" And then he laughed.

I responded, keeping my eyes closed, "Yeah, yeah, how much did we drink last night anyway?"

Don told me, "After the third trip to the club, it didn't matter anymore."

Holding my hand, I got up and dressed and then we made our way to breakfast. It wasn't easy to keep down, considering it consisted of under-cooked bacon and runny eggs when the yolks were punctured.

Back in the Hooch, I felt a lot better and Don began putting his package together for mailing. I decided to put one together myself, because I had a few things to mail home, too.

I found a box behind the supply building and filled it with a mosquito net with poles for my Father and one of the flare parachutes from our last mission for my Mother. Then I found a small plastic container which I put the negatives of Joe in it. Then I placed the container in the middle of the parachute. I then wrapped the box for mailing. In big letters, I wrote on the side of the box, "DESCRIPTION OF CONTENTS IS CLOTHES, PICTURES, AND NEGATIVES." The later was so the box wouldn't be X-rayed. Both finished, we headed for the Post Office.

When we got back from the Post Office, we went to check out the commotion in front of the C.O.'s office. We stopped beside Gary and I asked, "What's up?"

Gary responded, "Sergeant Baker's minesweeping team got ambushed. It seems they went out without much ammunition. Some only had a clip for their weapons. When their ammunition ran out, the ones not dead yet pretended to be. But the Vietnamese bayoneted them anyway before stripping them of everything including their clothes. We're now waiting to find out if anyone made it, for rumor has it that at least one survived and that's why they know what happened."

We all stood in silence now as the First Sergeant stepped out of his office to address us, "This incident didn't have to happen. At least not with these results. In the future, the orders are that anyone caught off company grounds for any reason without being fully armed, will be subject to disciplinary action. Now as to what you're waiting for: Sergeant Baker is dead. Along with Joe Wolf, Danny Woods, Melvin Dolor, Aaron Dutter and Anthony Myers. Seriously wounded and on the critical list are John Colburn, Joe Jackson, and Richard Simmons. The only one without a scratch was Paul Logan." Then he turned and reentered his office without further comment. We left in heavy thought.

That evening was spent in silence. When Paul came in, Don asked, "You okay, Paul?"

Paul shrugged and went to his cot. He got undressed, crawled in, and we all figured that was a good idea. We did the same. But I for one didn't sleep well.

I awoke to the sun shining hot, with the humidity still high. After breakfast, Sergeant Hicks came in announcing, "Okay men, you've rested long enough. Get your gear together. We're going up on a mountain for a few days to build some Bunkers."

As I got off my cot, Don asked, "Does it have a name?"

Hicks answered, "Matter of fact, it does. It's called 'Hill 270'. We leave in twenty minutes." And he left.

We got our gear and headed for the loading area. Besides Don and I, there was Jerry, Paul, Bud, Sal, and Rebel. We went by truck to the chopper pad, then by chopper to a mountain that was in the middle of a valley, which later I found out was called Dragon Valley.

I could see that from a plateau on top of a mountain we would be occupying, that the whole valley could be observed, making it an important strategic advantage point to hold.

It wasn't what I would have called a mountain, more like a large hill. Probably getting its name from its height. But in relation to the terrain of South Vietnam that I had seen, I could see them calling it a mountain.

The plateau was maybe seventy meters long by fifty or so meters wide and manned by six infantrymen, a four-man mortar team, whose mortar tube was positioned in the middle of the plateau.

There was only one Bunker completely finished and inside it was the last of the plateau's company consisting of two men operating what looked like a radar scope. But this one had wires running from it, out the door and down the hill to another wire which ran around the full base of the hill. I was told it would detect anything with body heat moving over it.

"Weaver!" A voice snapped me out of my daydream and turning around, it was Sergeant Hicks who called me. "Did you come out here to sightsee or work?"

I walked past him answering, "Is that a multiple choice question?" He didn't respond and I didn't pursue it.

Paul, Sal, and I worked on one Bunker, while Don, Bud, and Rebel worked on another. Jerry brought lumber and other material to both sites and we worked through the day. We stopped only when the chopper brought in hot food and cold drinks.

After dark, Sergeant Hicks volunteered us to give the infantrymen a break by pulling guard for them. I couldn't understand from what we were giving them a break. Because all they did was eat and sleep during the day and pull guard duty at night.

We were assigned two each to the four Bunker sites. One Bunker at each end and both sides of the plateau. There were only seven of us, so Hicks told us he would be pulling guard duty with Paul. But he said that he would be making rounds often to make sure there was a man awake at all times.

Bud and Don were assigned to the East side, Sal and Rebel the North, Jerry and I the West and Paul to the South. We got our gear, went to our assigned positions and soon we were settled in for the night.

Not feeling sleepy, I told Jerry, "I'll take the first watch and we'll play it by ear from there. Okay?"

"Suits me. I'll be asleep by the time my head hits the ground."And he was, too.

With such a bright moonlit night, I could see Jerry wasn't bothered by the rocky ground and figured he could sleep anywhere, anytime and under any conditions. I envied him. Before I came into the service, I was the same way, maybe even more so.

I heard footsteps coming and figured it was Hicks making one of his rounds. Sure enough, he whispered softly when close enough, "How are things here?"

I answered in a whisper: "Fine. Just enjoying that beautiful sky."

Sergeant Hicks sat down beside me, leaning back to imitate me, supporting myself on my elbows.

After a few minutes of looking up at the sky, he exclaimed, "You know something Weaver? This country is not only beautiful, but rich, too. It has almost everything you could find anywhere else in the world, but they would rather destroy it with war. What's even worse is that by the time they're finished, this will be the poorest country." He fell silent with that and I didn't say anything as we continued looking at the sky.

After a while, he said as he got up, "Stay alert." Then he left.

At 0140 hours, I shook Jerry awake and informed him, "It's time."

He got up stretching and after removing the rocks from where I would be lying, I settled down and soon was sound asleep.

When I woke up, it was breaking day and Jerry said, "You going to sleep all day? Come on, the breakfast chopper's coming."

We ate and then set to work, only stopping when the lunch choppers arrived. Even in the heat, the hot food was good.

As we finished eating, Paul pointed across the valley and said, "Look at those jets pounding that hill over there." We all went to the edge of the plateau to see.

Across the valley, jets were dropping long slender silver canisters that flipped end over end as they descended to the ground and vanished into the trees creating a large gray cloud that appeared above the trees.

Others emitted fireworks with streaks of fire reaching into the sky. I knew these were either Phosphorus and/or Napalm bombs.

The gray cloud forming over the trees got bigger with each new canister of that type. The slight breeze brought the cloud slowly down the mountain and across the valley floor toward us, as if it were alive.

Someone asked, "I wonder what kind of cloud that is?"

His last word was followed by Sergeant Hicks, shouting as he rushed off, "Get your gas masks on! That gas is about to engulf us." And we all ran for our masks.

I made it to mine just as the gas broke over us. My eyes started burning and I closed my eyes tight and held my breath. I finally got my gas mask on, cleared the airway and then opened my eyes. They burned even worse!

I sat down to debate whether to take my mask off or not. I finally decided to leave it on and hope the burning would ease soon.

It seemed to get hotter in the Bunker as more sweat seemed to fall into my eyes and burn even more. It also began to sting my skin. I rushed outside in hopes the moving air would ease things, but it didn't.

Everyone kept their masks on and time seemed to almost stop before Sergeant Hicks removed his mask. I, for one, anxiously hoped he wouldn't quickly put it back on.

As he lowered it to his side, I jerked mine off and took a deep breath. Though my eyes still burned and my skin stung, it was good having fresh air filling my lungs. It seemed to be that way for everyone else, too.

We all rushed to the water tank to wash our faces with the hope of easing our burning eyes and stinging faces. However, it only helped a little.

As we dried off, I exclaimed, "If that stuff was this strong here, I wonder what it was like over there? Not that I want to find out."

Sergeant Hicks replied, "It gets them out into the open. But you experienced it at its strongest when you were going through the gas chamber in training."

I just nodded, not wanting to tell him that I had pulled K.P. (Kitchen Police) washing dishes that day. I got out of having to go through it and this was my first experience at being gassed.

When the choppers brought in supper, the stinging and burning had diminished because of the heavy sweating of hard work we did.

We didn't have to pull guard duty once we finished the day. I laid down and was instantly sound asleep.

I was brought out of that sleep by an explosion close by. Instantly, I jumped up grabbing my weapon in the same movement and left the Bunker just as a mortar round left the tube outside the Bunker I had occupied.

I crawled on top of the Bunker and found Paul up there. I asked, "What's going on? Are we under attack?"

Paul explained, "We don't know. Something crossed the wire down below." The round just fired exploded and Paul fell silent as another round was sent on its way from the mortar tube.

What surprised me was the fact that the tube the mortars were being fired out of was pointing, what looked like straight up. But the rounds were missing the top of the hill somehow, landing and going off at the bottom of it.

After six rounds, the mortar team stopped and we all waited for the guys on the scope to report whether or not there was any more movement below.

When nothing happened after an hour, the scope watchers gave All the Clear and I went back to bed and sleep.

Morning came and by noon we had finished all the Bunkers. We climbed onto the choppers and headed for home. As we flew off, I looked back and felt the pride at the finished job we were leaving behind.

Back in the Hooch, we cleaned our gear and then showered. I felt great now, but the Hooch seemed to get smaller with each return to it.

Don and I walked around just killing time. As we passed the bulletin board, we stopped and checked it out. Then I discovered that I had to pull guard duty, and swore, "Damn!"

Don pointed further down the paper commenting, "If you look a little further, you'll find my name as well."

The night Sergeant Hicks addressed us, "I know you guys aren't happy about this. But we're short-handed and tomorrow I'll make sure you get plenty of rest. Maybe even go to the beach. But for now, load up, and pick your own teams for tonight." And we did.

Jerry asked to join Don and me and we welcomed him. When the truck stopped at the First Bunker, we quickly disembarked. In almost no time, we had everything set up on top of the Bunker. We settled back for the night and watched the small round boats that Don informed me were Vietnamese Sam Pan fishing boats. Now I had finally gotten to see one even it from a mile or so away. But there seemed to be literally thousands of them tonight and they were moving closer and closer to shore. And that was something that even we had heard was taboo near the Air Base for the Vietnamese.

I was listening to Don when suddenly there was a rustle in the brush out in front of the Bunker. All our attention shifted there, our weapons trained on it. Then we saw a small animal that I recognized as a Mongoose.

We sighed with relief because it was obvious the Mongoose was stalking something we couldn't as yet see.

Making a sudden dash into the brush, it quickly pulled out what, at first, looked like a rope. A second later, we instantly knew it was a snake, but not what kind.

As the Mongoose released the head of the snake, the other end whipped around, rose and the head flattened out, showing it was a Cobra.

The Mongoose circled the snake, now and then darting in and just barely escaping the Cobra's strike.

The show they put on was more spectacular than watching it on tv, which was the only place I'd ever seen anything like this before.

The sun went down as the two battled on. At one point, I was sure the Mongoose had been bitten, but soon realized it hadn't as its movements didn't slow down in the slightest.

As the twilight lingered on, we saw the Mongoose attack and as the snake struck, the Mongoose sidestepped. The snake's upper portion was stretched out and before it could recover, the Mongoose's body seemed to continue forward, while its head changed directions to bite the snake from behind, in the back of its head. Then hung on to it.

The rest of the Mongoose's body came around and the snake tried to coil around the head of the Mongoose. However, I knew it was over for the Cobra.

As the Mongoose dragged the snake off into the brush, Jerry was the first to speak, "I've never seen anything like that before! It was as if that animal was a pro at killing snakes and ..."

Don interrupted him with, "It's a Mongoose. They are pros at killing snakes." We settled back as Don asked, "How about you taking the first watch, Jerry? Ward and I are beat."

Jerry responded, "Sure. I got plenty of sleep today. I should be able to last most of the night."

I woke with a splitting headache and it was still dark. I saw a figure and asked, "Who's on watch?"

It was Jerry's voice answering, "Can't sleep?"

I replied, "That's not it. I've got this damned headache and nothing to take for it. I fell silent because the pain was now starting to throb behind my eyes.

Suddenly I thought my head was going to explode. No matter how hard I tried to get my mind off the pain, it just got worse.

Soon it was hurting so bad, I wanted to scream. But I knew that wouldn't do any good.

Jerry asked obviously concerned, "Is there anything I can do?"

Through gritted teeth, I told him, "Not unless you'll put your weapon to my head and pull the trigger!" I was serious, for the pain had me rolling on the Bunker.

I heard Jerry ask, "You want me to call for help?"

I didn't answer. I just asked, "What time is it?"

If he answered, I didn't hear him, because the pain had magnified so intensely, that time held no importance any longer. I just hoped to be strong enough to fight some of the pain off and not scream until the truck arrived.

I knew it was going to be hard though, for my head was about to the point where I was afraid it wouldn't explode and stop the pain.

When I was aware of things again, daylight must have come. I could hear the truck coming and then hands were helping me up and off the Bunker. I was no longer able to control myself and screamed as I kept my eyes closed as tight as possible. I just knew that if I opened them, my eyeballs would pop out of their sockets.

Someone helped me onto the back of the truck and I could hear a conversation going on around me. But I couldn't make out what they were saying, nor did I care.

The truck bounced along and I couldn't help the screams with which I filled the air. It felt like someone was trying to poke my eyes out with a red hot iron poker.

The trip down the mountain seemed rougher than usual and I did my best to control myself. But most of the time I failed.

The truck stopped and I was helped out of it. I was carried into a building and the smell told me I was probably in the infirmary.

When I was helped onto a hard table, I cried out, "Oh please, give me something for the pain! I can't stand it any longer!"

I heard a voice beside me say, "Give him a shot of Codeine."

Soon a needle was shoved into my left arm and whatever was shot into me stung. But if it stopped the pain, it would be worth it.

It seemed like an eternity of waiting. The pain just got worse and I couldn't keep another scream from escaping through my clenched teeth.

A hand touched me and a voice asked, "Isn't it easing son?"

I tried to get an answer out in one breath, but failed, "NO! It still...(gasp)... hurts like hell... (gasp)... give me something Doc...(gasp)... My head is exploding."

I heard the voice order, "Give him a shot or Morphine."

This time the needle went into my right arm and it seemed to stay there longer than the previous shot. But this time a warmth flowed over me, starting from the top of my head and slowly swept down over my body, washing the pain away.

By the time the needle was removed, the pain was washed away. I opened my eyes to the bright light overhead.

Squinting, I could see a man in white, standing beside me, and he asked, "Is the pain gone now?"

I exclaimed, smiling, "Oh yeah. Thanks, Doc. I feel great." And I started to get up.

The man placed a hand against my chest, preventing me from rising as he said, "Just lay there a while, son." And I relaxed, just thankful the pain had been taken away.

I asked, figuring he was in charge, "What happened to me?"

Before responding, he took out a pen, looked into my eyes and told someone behind him, "Get a pair of the darkest sunglasses from the back room." A few moments later, a pair of sunglasses with cardboard frames were put on me. Through them all I could see were silhouettes.

Now the Doctor told me, "Wear these during the day. As for what caused this, it has a long name. But simply put, you had a sinus attack with muscle spasms over your right eye. Your pupils dilated beyond their limits. More than I've ever seen before. It's a wonder you're not blind in at least your right eye. You still may become so if you don't keep those sunglasses on while you're out in the direct sun. I'm going to give you a prescription for Morphine and send you to the hospital for a week or so. We'll see if your eyes correct themselves in that time."

I told him, "But Doc, it doesn't hurt anymore. As a matter of fact, I've never felt better."

He responded, smiling, "That's because you're drugged. Once it wears off though, you'll be right back as you were when you came in."

I relaxed, knowing the Doctor was right. Two guys brought in a stretcher and the Doctor asked me, "Would you mind releasing your weapon now, since the pain is gone?"

I looked down and sure enough, there was my rifle. So I looked back at the Doctor asking, "Why didn't you take it?"

The Doctor chuckled and then answered, "Your friend tried, but you wouldn't release it to anyone. I decided not to force the issue, because I was afraid it might escalate into a more serious problem."

I replied, "Sorry. I guess it's my training." And I released my weapon to him, adding, "I'm trusting you to get this to my company for me, Doc."

He took my rifle answering, "I'll see it gets there."

I was put in the back of an ambulance and we drove off.

I heard a sound beside me and raising the sunglasses slightly, I saw two Americans also on stretchers. One was in the lower rack, the other in the upper, like me. I asked the one across from me, "How you doing?"

He replied, "Not good. We were wounded on a patrol and they're sending us to the hospital."

I asked, without thinking, "How bad is it?"

I didn't expect the response he gave me as he folded back his blanket, saying, "Bad enough, I guess." And in the dim light from the dome-light above us, I could see the gut bag tied around his waist, preventing the rest of his insides from falling out altogether.

I asked before thinking again, "Does it hurt much?"

He answered covering himself, "I can't feel a thing under the Morphine. The medic didn't want to give us anything. But I talked him into it anyway. What kind of wound did you get?"

Embarrassed now, I told him in a low voice, "No wound. They had to give me Morphine to kill the pain in my head. The Doctor said my eyeball about exploded in my head."

I stopped there, waiting for him to make a sarcastic remark. But he didn't. He just said, "I wondered about the shades, I thought you might be a star traveling in disguise." And we both laughed. With that, the fear was gone and he went on, "My name's Webster. What's yours?"

I told him, "Weaver, Glad to meet you." And we talked about back home and what all we were going to do when we got there.

The ambulance stopped and Webster was taken out first.

206

Then, his friend before I was taken to a long room where beds lined both sides of it.

After being placed in one of those beds, a Doctor came in, removed my sunglasses and checked my eyes with a pen-light.

After replacing the sunglasses, he left without a word. I laid there, enjoying the air-conditioned room and fell asleep.

I woke up hungry. So I asked the nurse, "Will we be eating soon?"

She replied, "In about twenty minutes."

With my sunglasses on, I couldn't make out much. I raised them a little and saw that she was a beautiful American woman.

The pain was returning, so I asked, "You got anything for the pain in my head?"

She came to the foot of the bed, picked up the clipboard hanging there and read it. She then told me, "Have you had anything since you arrived?"

I told her, "No." And she stormed off, swearing softly.

She brought me a pill and for the next seven days, I was given Morphine pills three times a day. Otherwise, I just ate and slept being checked by the Doctor several times a day.

On the seventh day, the Doctor told me, after examining my eyes, "You can go back to your company today. Just keep your sunglasses on for a couple more weeks. I'll give you a prescription, which you can use when needed, according to your pain."

"Yes, Sir," I answered and he wrote on a piece of paper and then giving it to me, he left the room.

I got dressed, feeling rather weak in the legs from being in bed so long.

I found the Pharmacy and filled my prescription before signing out of the hospital. Then I headed for the road home and lucked out catching a ride all the way to the front gate of my company.

I first reported to the commander before going to the Hooch. I found my weapon and gear lying on my cot. Cole was the only other person in the Hooch and he asked, "How are you feeling?"

"Great! But, where is everyone?"

"Out beating the bush. They left last night."

I put my rifle and gear away before lying down to rest. It was three days later before the squad came back in. They hadn't had any encounters with the VC, but as always, they were tired, wet, and dirty. After cleaning up and eating, they all went to bed. Don seeming to be taking steps to avoid me.

Before we went to bed, I asked, "How's it going, Don?"

Without looking at me, he replied, "Nothing." After that, I figured to just stay out of his way until I found out what his problem was.

I took a pill and kicked back for the rest of the night.

The next night as I laid on my cot, Don came over and sat on the cot across from me asking, "What's with you, Ward?"

I had no idea what he was talking about, so I inquired, "What do you mean?" And I wondered why he was so upset.

"I hear you've been shamming!"

I exclaimed, raising my voice in shock, "Shamming?" What in

the hell are you talking about? Who said I've been shamming?"

"It doesn't matter. But what does is that you need to tell me where you've been since leaving the Bunker over a week ago?"

"You mean you didn't come down the hill with me?"

"I couldn't. I wasn't going to leave Jerry to pull guard duty the rest of the night all alone. Besides all I knew is that I woke to Jerry telling me that you had a headache. He said he called for a truck that came and took you down the hill. Then I don't hear from you until I come in from the boonies. And here you are just laying around on your ass."

Now I understood what was going on. I explained what had happened. Then asked, "Then why didn't you send word?"

"How could I?" I said, "The only people I saw the whole time I was there were Doctors and nurses. And they didn't exactly have phone service there. But look who's talking about sending word! When you got hit, why didn't you send word to me? You at least knew I was alive! I didn't have the pleasure of knowing that about you!"

I guess maybe he sensed the anger in my voice. "Because," he shrugged a little, "for the same reason you didn't," he said.

I relaxed somewhat before speaking, "Next time ask in advance. Now, how about you try one of these?" And I handed him my bottle of pills.

He read the label and smiled. Then he opened the container and took one out. I figured things were back to normal between us.

The squad wasn't due to go out for several days and the Sergeant was going to keep his word. The next morning, the

Captain announced that after breakfast, the company was going to the beach.

We loaded up in the trucks and soon were parked next to the ocean. Like several others, I went directly out into the surf with my inflated air mattress and I truly enjoyed myself.

When I got hungry, I got a plate of food and a soft drink; then I went to the shade where I enjoyed eating.

Afterwards, I found Don, telling him I needed more pills. So he left with me and soon we found the Pharmacy. I now had more pills and we made it back to the beach in time to catch the trucks before they headed back to the company compound.

Back in the Hooch, Paul was packing and I asked him, "Going on R&R?"

Paul smiled big and announced, "No. I'm going home. My year's up today."

I was happy for him as he finished. I picked up his duffle bag, Don grabbed the box Paul had his extra things in and we escorted him to sign out. Then Don asked, "What time does your plane lift off?"

Paul answered, "Around two this afternoon."

At the office, Gary was there signing out to leave as well. I asked him, "Why didn't you tell me you were going home?"

Gary replied, "You'll understand when you get short."

The jeep came to take them to the airstrip, Paul and I shook hands, and he told me, "Ward, you're a fool around explosives. You don't seem to have nerve whatsoever handling the stuff. So if the gooks don't get you, I have no doubt you'll make it home."

I told him, "Thanks, I'll do my best. But how would you and Gary like to have some of these to get you off the ground with?"

I handed him my bottle of Morphine and when they both saw what it was, they said almost simultaneously, "How much?"

I responded, "I asked you if you wanted some, not if you wanted to buy any. You both know me better than that."

They both took two, swallowing one now, and then they loaded up and were off.

At 1400 hours, several of us were standing out away from the structure as a traditional farewell to anyone going home. Even though from the plane, it was very unlikely they could see us. We would see their plane after it left ground. They would know we were there sending them off.

We heard the engines roar and then it died out. Then it raced again and this time we could hear it roar down the runway. We waited to see it rise above the trees which prevented us from seeing it speed down the runway.

As the sound of the engines got louder, telling us it was quickly approaching liftoff, there was an explosion on the airstrip. We all looked at each other as another explosion happened seconds later and all eyes were now glued to the treetops knowing the airstrip was being hit by mortars.

Someone said lowly as another explosion went off: "Come on... get off the damn ground... rise, damn it!" His words were echoing everyone's thoughts.

A sigh of relief could be heard among us as the plane rose above the trees. But it was short lived as the plane exploded seconds later.

Horror filled everyone, knowing a mortar had hit the plane,

turning it into a ball of fire as burning pieces of it seemed to go in different directions.

Everything seemed to stop or move in slow motion as the plane settled below the treetops and out of our sight. Then a big explosion occurred. A ball of smoke and fire rose above the treetops and we all stood there awestruck and silent.

Sometime later, everyone started to move off still in silence.

The rest of the day was spent in the same way, even during supper. I wondered how a guy could come over, do the very best he could do, and never hurt anyone. Yet, he gets killed leaving the ground on his way back home?"

That night we started playing cards, trying to get our minds off the plane. After about two hours, the atmosphere started changing, and even laughter stirred the air.

Suddenly there was a heavy plunk sound across the floor and a popping sound blended in, without seeing what it was, fear swept over me, and my head snapped around. I saw a grenade rolling across the floor without a handle. No word was exchanged as I dove headfirst through the screen part of the wall and so did everyone else. I hit the ground hard, even though it was sand. Then an explosion followed from inside the Hooch, while I covered my head with both arms.

I laid there, not hurting anywhere, except for where I hit the ground. I wondered why and knew I was alive, only because the floor of the Hooch was made of two by twelves and was about three feet above the ground. It had absorbed the blast and shrapnel. I hoped our fast thinking had saved everyone.

As I got up, I saw the others rising as well. There was a lot of commotion as people rushed to assist us.

Someone found us and after yelling he had found us he asked, "What happened here? Is everyone okay?"

I followed the guys back inside. This time through the door as lamps were brought in to light up the place so we could assess the damage.

I heard Don exclaim angrily, "Shit! Some son-of-a-bitch is dead when I find out who threw that grenade in here!"

This was my thought exactly, as it was probably the others' as well. I added, "Was anyone hurt in the Hooch on either side of us?"

One of the guys answered, "No one was hurt. Everyone was either on guard or at the movie."

Nothing in the Hooch was salvageable. Everyone set to work cleaning the place out and supply opened so we could get cots and bedding. The rest would be gotten in the morning.

Soon, everyone left and we went to bed. I couldn't get to sleep and I wondered if Don was. So I asked low, "Don?"

He responded, "Yeah!"

I asked, "Have you any ideas as to who did this?"

"I don't. But I'll find out!"

I vowed as we fell silent to help and sleep overtook me some-time during the night.

The next morning we were issued all new gear and we set to work cleaning our new weapons and other gear, then put them away.

Some went to work, patching the holes in the Hooch, while others got the electricity back in the place. We had to install all new lights and plug-ins.

It was almost 2300 hours when we finished, so everyone went to bed, calling it a night.

I woke in the middle of the night to someone moving around in the Hooch. My head was spinning. But I leaned over, picked up my M-16 and when I slammed a round into the chamber, the figure froze, I asked, "Who are you and what are you doing in here?"

The guy never moved as he replied, "I'm a replacement. I just got assigned to this Hooch. My name's Charlie Summons."

I put my rifle down, got up, and turned the lights on. Charlie still hadn't moved. So I apologized, "Sorry about that. We had some excitement earlier, as you can see from the holes. We're still a little bit jumpy around here."

Don stirred and asked, "What's going on?" Charlie took one of the empty cots and I introduced Charlie to Don. Then I told Don about Charlie's earlier welcoming from me.

The next evening, I pulled guard duty with Jerry and James. It started off quietly and we took our turns sleeping. Later I woke and found Jerry on watch. I didn't know why I woke up, but I got up, went to the window and asked, "Jerry, can I look through the scope? I have an odd feeling."

He gave me the scope and I scanned the area, but I saw nothing moving, except fireflies.

I was about to give up when I saw a small movement. I focused the scope on it and saw that there was a large boulder about sixty meters out. A Vietnamese soldier was crawling on top of it. I lowered the scope and told Jerry softly, "Wake up, James."

He went to do that as I looked through the scope again. The

soldier was now sitting on top of the boulder, cross-legged, with his rifle lying across his lap as he smoked a cigarette.

Jerry came back with James asking, "What's out there?"

I replied, "There's a gook out there. I'm going to call it in. I just want you to confirm it first. I only saw one, but there could be more." And I gave him the scope.

Jerry took it and after a few seconds of looking through it, he exclaimed, "There he is, big as day. He's either brave or stupid. I'm not sure which. "

I picked up the phone, spun the crank, and a voice asked, "What's your situation?"

I explained what I saw and that Jerry confirmed it before I called. I requested permission to fire. The voice replied, "Permission granted. Heads up for the rest of you and good luck." Then I hung up the phone.

I took the scope for another look and James commented, "Some nerve. Of course, without the scope, we wouldn't have been able to tell his cigarette from all the fireflies. Damn!"

James was right. I told him, "Get your M-79 ready. You'll fire first and then we'll open up." He nodded and we got ready.

When we heard the pop of James' M-79 launcher go off. I opened fire with the sixty and Jerry fired his M-16.

I ran off about fifty rounds before stopping. Then I told the others, "Ceasefire."

They did and I picked up the scope, looking the boulder over. But then, to my surprise, I saw the Vietnamese crawl back up on top of the same boulder. He sat down, laid his weapon across his lap and seemed to be watching me watch him.

None of the other Bunkers had fired, so I figured they hadn't found a target. I told the guys, "You're not going to believe this, but either the same gook or another one is crawling on top of that same boulder."

Jerry spoke, almost losing control of his volume, "What?" And he took the scope from me, taking a look for himself.

Jerry laid the scope down and commented angrily, "We won't miss this time!" I heard the pop of the handle of a grenade and saw him throw it out the window. We waited and when it went off, we all opened fire again.

I ran off about another fifty rounds, before stopping. When we looked through the scope this time, there was nothing moving, nor did anyone crawl back on top of the boulder. We couldn't see any other movement anywhere else.

After about fifteen minutes, I called it in, "Everything's still."

The voice replied, "In the morning, go out and confirm the kill." And the line went dead, so I hung up.

I stayed with the scope the next hour before feeling sleepy. I told the others, "You guys can take over. I'm getting some sleep." And I handed the scope to Jerry.

James responded, "It's my watch anyway. If Jerry wants to get some sleep as well?"

The next morning, I woke and Jerry told me, "James went to check things out. You're not going to believe this. We missed him, or them, altogether! There's no bodies, not even any blood!"

I exclaimed jumping up, "Can't be! He checked the wrong boulder." I grabbed my rifle, then I rushed out of the Bunker as James and Jerry covered me through the window.

I found the boulder and found Jerry was right. There was

nothing except several cigarette butts scattered beside the rock and marks made by the grenade and our shooting.

Back in the Bunker, I picked up the phone as Jerry said, "I already called it in."

I thanked him, thinking that if my father ever found out about this, he'd never let me hear the end of it.

No one said a word about it on the ride down the hill for which I was thankful. Once back in the Hooch, I cleaned up and we all went to breakfast.

* * *

That afternoon, Sergeant Hicks came around to tell us, "Get your gear ready, men. We're going out on patrol tonight. Pack to be out for several days. We leave at 1800 hours.

"Even Charlie?" I asked as the Sergeant turned to leave.

Sergeant Hicks declared, looking at me over his shoulder, "He might as well get his feet wet. Tonight's as good a time as any." And he left with no further word.

We all got packed, even helped Charlie with his and I was thankful to the guys who took Gary's place in supply for replacing all my clips. At the ammo Bunker, we loaded up with bandoleers, grenades and C-4.

Back in the Hooch, cases of C-rations had been brought in, and we loaded up our packs. Finally, we were ready to go.

At 1800 hours, we were in front of the CO's Office. Don and I were walking alongside Sergeant Hicks. Behind us were Charlie, Rebel, Phil, Del, Jerry, and Sam. Leading us all was a Captain, whom Sergeant Hicks introduced to us, "This is Captain Capps and he's going out with us. He has a lot of experience, having been here almost three complete tours. So listen to him and you may come back in one piece."

Now the Captain spoke, "For the rest of this mission, rank is dropped. You will call me Capps. I don't want the gooks knowing you have an officer in the field with you. We don't have time for questions. Just trust me and my experience. I've reviewed your files and I have complete faith in your abilities. As much as you're Sergeant has. Otherwise, I wouldn't be going out with you."

We loaded up and everyone was busy with their own thoughts. I wondered what kind of mission called for the dropping of rank. And what were my abilities that I was picked for this mission?

After dark, the trucks stopped and I had no idea where we were. Of course, I hadn't been paying that much attention either. We got out of the truck and everyone gathered around Captain Capps and Sergeant Hicks, waiting for further orders.

The Captain spoke softly, "Check your equipment as I call off what you should have so you don't carry excess weight. We're going to be traveling fast. Anything you want to leave, stow it in the truck." And then he started reading from a clipboard. I checked my pack as he went down the list. I had a pair of socks he didn't mention, but that was okay. I was keeping them.

When he said C-rations, someone whose voice I didn't recognize spat out, "Damn! That's what I forgot." Just about everyone snickered.

Sergeant Hicks interjected, "Get some from the front seat, Sam."

Everyone waited. It was too dark to see anything but silhouettes now. Sam finally exclaimed, "Got em Cap... I mean Capps."

Next, the Captain asked, "R.T.O, do you have extra batteries?"

Rebel answered, "Yes, Sir."

Then the Captain continued, "Okay. Single file. Keep the guy in front of you in sight. I'll lead, then Hicks."

As they moved out, I asked, "Don, where are you?" I had lost track of him.

His voice came from behind me, "Right here." he said.

I told him, "Then lead the way so I can keep an eye on you." He walked out ahead of me, responding in passing, "Yes, Mother."

I waited until I could hardly make out his silhouette and then started out with a few guys following me. I was very thankful for that.

We did travel fast for night maneuvers. After we traveled for what I figured to be a couple of miles, nothing had happened, which I was thankful for. But I still wondered how much further we had to go.

Suddenly I saw Don's arm motion me forward. I did the same to the men behind me and then I moved up.

Seconds later, we were all grouped and Capps whispered to us, "The following men take your packs off: Rebel, Don, Del, and Ward. The rest of you spread out and give them cover."

As the others spread out, we slipped out of our packs. Captain Capps now told us, "There's a camp of hardcore regulars ahead with four sentries. Hicks told me you four have the necessary hunting skills to take out the sentries. Here..." And he gave each of us a coil of wire, that when stretched out, with its short dowel at each end, was a garrote.

Knowing what we had to do, Don was sent off to the far left; rebel the next one closer, Del to the one just right of us and I was sent to the far right one. Just like the other men, I moved out toward my quarry, keeping focus on remembering the training my father had given me. Much of it was self-taught while deer hunting.

During the heat of the day, when the bucks bed down and the does feed freely, dad and I would find a doe eating. Then spread out behind her, we would see who could get the closest before she looked at the one of us she'd heard and then she would bolt off into the foliage.

I was only meters from the silhouette, not sure if he was facing me or not. If he was facing me, the shooting would start.

There was no way I would be able to get to him in time.

I took a deep breath, then slowly let it out. Then I continued to breathe shallowly through my open mouth. It wouldn't be heard as easily as breathing through my nose.

I kept my body relaxed and alert as I slowly moved closer. A few feet away, I stopped. Suddenly, a slight noise came from the camp and the sentry almost facing me, twisted his body to look back in the direction of the camp. I laid my rifle down, seized the opportunity to make a loop in the garrote. I stepped up beside the sentry and dropped the looped wire over his head. Before he could react, I snapped my left hand out away from me as hard as I could. At the same time, I yanked my right hand back towards me equally fast and as hard.

He dropped his weapon, bringing both hands up to claw at the wire cutting through everything in his throat, except his spinal cord.

For a couple of seconds, the only sound heard was the scuffling of his feet. He was dead before his legs buckled, his clawing at the wire stopped, then his body-weight dropped. I slowly eased his body to the ground, looking toward the camp to see if anyone had heard anything. It had seemed to me like we had made enough noise to be heard beyond the camp. But nothing moved. I released the garrote and left it around his neck. I located his weapon and moved it further away from his body. Then I slowly eased back the way I came, picking up my rifle in passing.

I found my way back to Capps and Hicks, finding Rebel and Del already there. We waited for Don to return as well.

It wasn't long before he was back and I was relieved as we helped each other put our packs back on. Rebel was assisted with the radio and Captain Capps told us, "Plug the holes you guys made in the sentry line and I want this camp captured if possible. Regardless, but let no one escape! Now move out." And we did.

I moved back over the same ground I had just traveled, knowing it better. Soon I found myself back next to the body I had left. I lowered myself to one knee, raised my rifle, and rested my elbow on my other knee for support for my weapon. I waited as I watched the camp.

Soon I heard Captain Capps' voice speak in Vietnamese. Not understanding any of what he was saying, I figured he was probably telling them to surrender.

The figures in the camp scrambled and brought their weapons up to bare. But they didn't fire, nor did we as Captain Capps raised his voice, seeming to try and reason with them to not fire.

As he stopped talking, I saw one of the soldiers easing back toward the trees away from us. I called out, "One's trying to slip away."

I didn't fire, but kept my sight trained on him. Before Captain Capps could reply, the guy I was watching quickly brought his weapon up to fire in the direction of Capps. I knew there wasn't time to warn him, so I fired.

The man fired his weapon into the air as he fell. This started a chain reaction. Everyone started shooting on both sides.

The shooting only lasted what seemed like minutes. Then no

one in the camp moved. We waited, my nerves jumping like crazy inside me, my mind reeling, and I knew my adrenaline was pumping faster than a runaway locomotive. I wanted to scream, but kept myself in check.

Soon Captain Capps broke the silence, "Every other man from me check for wounded."

I waited to see if the man to my right moved out to know whether I was to go. He did, so I kept watch intently.

With only the light from three small fires, I couldn't make out who the four figures were going from body to body checking them. But I recognized Rebel's voice calling out, "Got one still breathing."

Captain Capps moved to Rebel who was kneeling before a wounded man. I couldn't hear anything, but I assumed Capps was questioning the wounded man.

After a while, Captain Capps stood asking in a normal voice, "Okay, who fired that first shot?"

I walked into the clearing and up to him. Then I answered, "I did. He was drawing a bead on you and I didn't think there was time to warn you. So I shot him. If I hadn't, we may not be standing here with you about to chew my ass out."

All Captain Capps said to that was, "Okay." Then he turned back to the wounded man as Rebel announced, "He's dead, Capps."

Captain Capps only hesitated a second before informing us, "Okay, let's move out. Same orders as before." And then we turned, heading the same general direction we had been traveling.

We'd only moved maybe a hundred meters when suddenly bullets were whistling by me. I hit the ground and saw Don's silhouette do the same. But I didn't know if he was okay until I saw his rifle fire. Then I looked for a target and started shooting.

I saw several flashes from weapon muzzles. So I emptied my clip at one and then another at a new target.

Men screamed in pain and agony, while others yelled for medics. But the shooting from both sides went on.

I emptied one clip after another, changing targets often. I was thankful for having the extra clips, as muzzle flashes became further and further apart, then the shooting slacked off. I hoped this signified the Vietnamese were withdrawing or dead.

I still had six full clips and took this time to reload my empties as all the shooting stopped as abruptly as it had started.

It was still too dark to see anything, so I stayed put, wishing it would hurry up and become daylight.

Captain Capps called out, "Sound off, everyone."

I spoke right up, "Weaver here." Don sounded off next and then Del, Jerry, and Rebel.

After a few moments of silence, Hicks announced, "Let's find the others and hope they're not too bad." And we set out searching.

Rebel found Phil and Hicks found Sam. Both Sam and Phil were dead. But Charlie was nowhere to be found. It was as if he had just vanished. We didn't know whether he had broken and run or if he was carried off by the Vietnamese. He was just Missing in Action (MIA).

Phil and Sam's bodies were stripped of identification, then wrapped in poncho liners and left for retrieval later.

We moved out and daylight found us exhausted.

When we came to a bluff, at the edge of the timberline, we stopped for the day to eat. Almost everyone slept, except for those taking turn to pull guard duty. Don took first watch.

I pulled my turn, but the day passed uneventful.

Just before dark, we were brought together and for the first time, I saw Captain Capps' arm bandaged and knew he must have been wounded during last night's fire-fight. But which one?

Now Capps informed us, "We'll move out a half hour after dark. Shortly after that, we should come upon what we came out here to find. It's a heavily traveled trail the Vietnamese use to bring mortars and other supplies down from Northern Vietnam. But tonight, they'll be walking into an ambush. Ours."

Don and I kicked back and I inquired, "Why can't ambushes be during the day so they don't interfere with sleep?"

"Sometimes they are. But take last night's action, if it had been day, we all would be dead now." I saw the logic of this.

Just before 1900 hours, we moved out and right where the Captain said it would be, we set up our ambush with lots of claymores. Hicks, Jerry, and I were placed on the west side of the trail, spread out ten meters apart. Capps, Don, Rebel, and Del went on the other side and once prepared, we started our wait. Something you learn to do well in the service: Wait!

The hours dragged on and several times I fought to keep from nodding off. I wished I had brought my Morphine, but not for any pain.

The sound of walking brought me out of my daydream and I

knew our waiting was finally over. It could only be the Vietnamese we were waiting for.

My rifle came up to the ready as a thought occurred, 'With us split on both sides of the trail and the enemy about to be between us, we could shoot each other tonight.' But then I realized Captain Capps and Sergeant Hicks surely knew this too. They must have compensated by placing us where it wouldn't happen.

We had been taught ambushes in training, but nothing out here seemed to be as we were taught.

The moon seemed to be out extra bright tonight and as the first silhouette passed me, the first shot rang out.

As the silhouette that had just passed me dropped his bundle from his shoulder, I fired and he joined his bundle on the ground, dead.

They had come in single file and I changed my aim. Claymores went off and there was screaming of pain as the air was filled with red and green tracers streaking across the jungle.

No longer able to see silhouettes due to their shooting from prone positions, I directed my firing toward the ground along the trial.

Time seemed to stand still during the fire-fight and then I heard Sergeant Hicks yell, "CEASE FIRE!" And we did.

As I waited for further orders, I gathered my empty clips, refilling them while I could. All the time scanning the area in front of me for any movement.

I was in the middle of filling a clip when I saw movement on the trail. I figured the movement was some soldier moving back into the brush. I dropped the clip I was reloading, grabbed my rifle, and emptied a clip at the movement. Then I finished filling my clips.

The waiting now started getting to me and my mind started running wild. I began imagining the enemy bellying towards me. Though the moon was bright, as brushy as it was, would I see them in time? I doubted it and what if the others were dead? I hadn't heard them fire when I just had. I hoped it was crazy thinking. But what if it wasn't?

I had spent many days alone in the woods back home, so this wouldn't have normally been a problem and I tried to keep my mind concentrating on the ambush.

Morning came without another incident and I saw Rebel appear on the trial going from body to body, checking what I suspected was for anyone still alive. He didn't find any.

Soon Captain Capps and Sergeant Hicks revealed themselves. The rest of us followed and found there had been fourteen men and two women dead in black pajamas. They had been carrying an ample supply of mortars, ammunition, food, and medical supplies.

Taking inventory of our group, no one had gotten even a scratch from the enemy. We set to work placing the supplies the Vietnamese had been carrying in a pile. Captain Capps allowed us to take some of the rations they carried to try later. Don placed the explosives and lit the fuse as we found cover.

After the pile exploded to bits and pieces, I hoped we would be heading for home now. That didn't prove to be the case, as Captain Capps announced as he gathered us around him, "You men probably want to go in now. But we did such a good job, I feel we can do one more night of damage before going home."

Rebel commented low, but I heard him, "If we live through another night!" And I chuckled agreeing with him.

Captain Capps continued as if not knowing he had been interrupted, " So tonight, we'll set up an ambush further up the trail. In the meantime, rest and eat."

Night came and we moved up the trail, again Captain Capps leading us.

Don was still walking ahead on my right. I was bringing up the rear this time.

The night went slow and several hours later, we stopped and grouping around Capps. Hicks whispered that point had just revealed a small village ahead with a few sentries. It must be a VC village.

Easing closer, when we were in sight of the village, Captain Capps had us spread out and take up positions around the village, which we did.

It was slow going with the moon so bright again tonight.

I moved off to the right, walking slowly. The brush was really thick making it really slow-going.

It also seemed to me noisier than it should have been. I wasn't sure we could get very close to the village without being heard. But I kept going, though, trying to be as quiet as possible.

When I arrived at the place I was to be, surprised at not yet having been detected. I lowered myself to one knee and placed my elbow on my other knee for the rifle support and waited. I watched the sentry in front of me. I waited to see what happened next, for we had orders not to fire until Capps did.

An eternity passed and it slowly got light. I figured the waiting for daylight was the delay. But it had been a torture to me watching that sentry smoking cigarettes. The smoke drifted my way and I wanted one real bad. It seemed like days since my last one and I could almost taste the one he was smoking.

All of a sudden, I heard a rustling behind me and I spun quickly, ready to shoot, if needed. In the twilight before dawn, I could make out Rebel behind a Vietnamese soldier, just feet behind me.

Rebel's hand was covering the man's mouth. The way the soldier's body was quivering, I knew Rebel had shoved his bayonet inside the man's back, twisting it.

As Rebel lowered the man to the ground, I quickly turned back to see if the sentry had heard anything. But apparently he hadn't, for he was lighting another cigarette and I wanted to shoot him for that, if for no other reason.

I turned my head back to give Rebel a thumbs up for saving my life. But there was no one there. I figured Rebel must have made his way back to where he was supposed to be. So I would thank him later and went back to watching the sentry.

A shot rang out at the far side of the village from me. As the sentry turned toward the sound bringing his weapon off his shoulder, I squeezed off a round. He went down dead.

It was full light now as shooting was coming from every direction. Someone exited a hut, but before he could fire his weapon, someone else did and the man went down as well.

The Vietnamese started bursting through walls of huts. Everyone opened fire, people ran in various directions as I emptied one clip after another, working automatically, almost out of fear.

When there were no more targets, the shooting stopped and

we moved in to search the place. We couldn't find anything except weapons with most of the bodies.

Captain Capps assured us that we were only a few miles from our pick-up point. Trucks were already on their way there. We headed out, but cautiously, because we were sure some Vietnamese had escaped and may be waiting in ambush for us.

The journey to the trucks was a long and slow process, but we made it without incident. Soon we were loaded up and heading for home. In route we found out Phil and Sam had been picked up, but a search of the area didn't turn up any sign of Charlie.

I found Rebel and thanked him for saving my life. He smiled responding, "Ah, you're welcome. I just saw that sneaky bastard going through the brush, as intent on you..." Rebel snickered as he went on, "...that he didn't hear me trip going through the brush getting to him. He must have thought you were lost and out there alone."

The next day, I found my name on the guard duty list. I just sat quietly, feeling sorry for myself. I was puzzled as to why I was still alive.

People all around me had died since my losing the lumber yard, but I was still without a scratch. Why? I had come over here to die and I didn't consider myself a coward anymore, but then too, I wasn't a hero. I had never been especially lucky. So why was I still alive? I laid on my cot feeling like a prisoner within my own body and thoughts.

After a while, I couldn't stand just lying there, beating myself up. I got up and went outside, walking aimlessly, searching for answers. When they didn't come, I got my bottle of Morphine and took a couple.

I was down to my last pill, so I caught a ride to the main post.

At the Pharmacy, I was told by the Pharmacist, "You're going through too many pills. If you're still in that much pain, you'd better go see the Doctor."

I still had the prescription the Doctor at the infirmary had given me. I could go to another druggist, but decided against it.

I had stopped wearing the sunglasses the Doctor had given me. Instead, I was wearing a pair I had bought at the PX. But I didn't want to give up my pills.

Remembering Williams, from the Special Forces, with the Navy that I had helped out with sandbags on several occasions when he didn't have paperwork and had taken me fishing. He had said if I ever needed anything to look him up again. So I went to their place behind the USO Club and shortly was knocking on the door of his Hooch.

He answered it and we shook hands as he greeted me cheerfully. "How are you doing? Come to do a little fishing again? The boat..."

I interrupted, "As much as I'd love that, I can't. Not today. But I do need your help."

"Want something cold to drink?" I nodded and followed him to an icebox where he took out two beers, handing me one and then said as we opened them, "Who you want dead?"

I chuckled knowing he wasn't really joking. But I explained, "Do you have any of those fifty-five-gallon survival drums around?"

He asked in surprise, "How do you know about them?"

I explained, "A month before I turned seventeen, I joined the Navy reserves without a physical and was in for three months before they found out I had a bad ticker. I was kicked out, which is another story before you ask. But while I was in, I learned what was in them and particularly the package at the top."

Williams smiled asking, "You mean the self-injector Morphine packs?" I nodded and he added, "No problem, how many you want?"

"I don't have any mon..."

He quickly interrupted me, "You finish that sentence and you're out of here empty handed!" I smiled nodding.

He led me across the compound to a small building, saying as he opened the door, "We'll call it a favor between two fishermen."

"Thanks, Williams. I'll take as many as I can get."

We entered the structure where there was at least twenty barrels. Williams popped the lid off one saying, "Help yourself. Take what you want."

I looked and to my amazement, the barrel was full of nothing but self-injector Morphine and I started filling all my pockets as Williams asked, "Do you mind my asking what they're for? Are you finally going into business?"

I explained about being hooked and needing them and why I got this way. He understood. He inquired when I finished loading my pockets, "If you can't get enough in your pockets, I'll get you a sack?"

I told him that wasn't necessary adding, "That is if I need more, can I..."

He waved me off, interjecting, "You come back anytime you want, for fishing or whatever. You're always welcome."

We went back to his Hooch, where we shook hands. I thanked him again and left.

I caught a ride to the front gate of my company and back in the Hooch, I first emptied my pockets into my footlocker.

I kept one self-injector out. I took the cover off the needle, squeezed the plastic tube so there wasn't any air in the needle, and then realized I still couldn't inject myself even after all these years.

I wished I'd gotten Williams to have given me one earlier.

Don came in and I held the self-injector behind my back, but stayed sitting on my cot and said, "You look down, buddy. Lose anything?"

Don inquired, "Didn't you hear about what happened to the three guys in Fourth Platoon, First Squad while we were gone?"

I shook my head informing him, "I just got back from the Main Post a few minutes ago. What happened?"

"Well, it seems they were sleeping in their Hooch, someone came in and...Well, they were found the next morning with their throats cut. No one saw or heard anything. But what's worse is, they're not sure it was even the gooks that did it. It may have been one of our own."

I slammed my free hand down on my mattress, "Probably the same bastard that tossed the grenade in here that night!" I said heatedly. Don just nodded.

I didn't know what else to say as I looked around, knowing now that even here I wasn't safe. A cold chill ran through me. Looking at Don, I suggested, "Look in my footlocker. See if there's anything that might help you through this?"

I watched him go in the locker and then he whistled low before saying, "I don't mind if I do." He took one of the Morphine modules out, closed the lid on the footlocker and came back sitting on my cot adding, "Thanks, this should do nicely for a while. But when did you start shooting up?"

As I told him, he injected himself, squeezing the tube empty. I finished by asking him to inject me and why, which he was happy to do. Afterward, neither of us felt disappointed or frustrated about anything.

Two days later, we were told to get ready to go out on a 'Search And Destroy Mission.' But we weren't told where or as to how many days we could expect to be gone.

The time for our departure came and we fell out with all gear, as did most of the other squads. The number of us was an amount I hadn't seen going out on a mission at one time since our trip onto the peninsula during the "Tet Offensive."

Sergeant Hicks came out of the office and addressed us, "Men, we're going to be attached to a Cavalry unit this time. So we'll be riding all the way. They'll be here any second to pick us up. This time, I don't know any more than you do, except that the person in charge will be a Captain Carson. But we can deal with whatever comes, can't we engineers?"And there was a roar of agreement.

Soon we heard the tracks coming and we grabbed our gear. They came into view and stopped in front of us. There were eight APC's and one tank with a ninety-millimeter cannon sticking out of its turret. A Captain, from the hips up, was standing within the opening at the top of the turret, looking like a picture I'd once seen of General Patton.

The engines didn't turn off, but we were motioned to mount

up. We climbed aboard and soon were on our way down Highway One heading North.

It was a pretty smooth going, considering until several hours later, we turned West off Highway One and headed across the rice paddies at almost full speed.

My backpack started hurting my shoulders. So I took it off and slipped it under me to sit on. Then I hung onto whatever I could to keep from being bounced off the top of the APC.

We finally made camp in a small clearing. I was happy to be off that bucking metal animal. I just wanted to rest. But before that could happen, Don and I found ourselves pulling a shift of guard duty.

Before pulling it, knowing we wouldn't be doing it together, Don injected us both and we went on duty free of frustration or cares of any kind.

Sometime during the night, a shot rang out. It brought me out of the slumber I was in. Then a lot of shooting followed all around me. I thought all hell had broken loose as I grabbed my rifle and gear, crawled toward the APC feeling totally unorganized.

Instead of an APC, I found myself behind a big rock. So I laid my head against it for a moment to gather my senses as bullets whizzed past the rock I was behind.

Once my head had cleared, I used the rock as a shield. I raised my weapon over it and peeking over it as well, looked for a target. It wasn't hard to find the flash of a weapon from the woods, so I picked one and emptied a clip at it.

That flash stopped and I picked another spot putting a new clip in my weapon. Then I emptied it at the next muzzle flash.

Shooting got heavy as red and green tracers crisscrossed the air like a spider web that seemed to let nothing escape as men screamed and yelled from pain and agony on both sides. And no matter how hard I tried to close my ears to it, I couldn't.

As I was loading clips, having run them all out, the command came to cease fire. It slowly did and I continued filling my clips, wondering where Don was.

I called out, not caring about being quiet. I fully knew that we were supposed to be quiet in a situation like this, but I didn't care. "Don! You okay?"

Don responded from behind an APC not far away. "I'm okay. Just keep your head down. It's not over yet."

We fell silent and waited as I now had all my clips loaded. Dawn came with no more shooting. I saw the medic moving from place to place, making sure everyone was okay. When he came to me, he asked, "Everything alright?"

I answered, "Yeah, Doc. How about everyone else?"

He told me, "So far, so good." Then he moved on to the next guy. I felt better with this news as I had him to cover.

The sun got hot quick and the command to group up came. I came out from behind my rock, joining Don and together we followed the others.

When the Captain immerged from his tank, he told us, "Load up. There's a village nearby here that we're going to visit. But be ready. It's a VC village." And we all loaded up with my wondering how he knew it was a VC village?

The APC's and tank stopped just outside the village and everyone dismounted the APC's, except the gunners. Now we followed the APC's the rest of the way to the village, ready for anything.

Several APC's spread out on one side of the village while others went around to the other side spreading out there.

The people in the village gave no resistance. Hearing us coming, they huddled together in the middle of the village and I could see the fear on their faces. Most of the group consisted of old men, women, and children. I didn't see a single weapon among the lot of them.

As the huts were searched, Captain Carson spoke in Vietnamese to the villagers and I got enough to know he was ordering them into the large community hut in the middle of the village or be shot and most of them complied quickly.

Captain Carson approached an old man who was refusing to comply. The Captain took hold of the old man's shirt and raising him off the ground, spoke harshly to him. I figured he was now asking the old man about VC in the area.

When the old man shook his head, Captain Carson gave the old man the back of his hand slapping him across the face and let the old man slump to the ground still holding his shirt and continuing to slap the guy over and over, even after blood appeared in the corner of the old man's mouth and nose.

Appearing to tire, the Captain spoke English to the medic standing close by, "Hey Doc, come here."

The medic approached him asking, "What do you want, Sir?"

Captain Carson answered, "I think this guy wants to talk to you out behind the hut. Take him out there and see what you can find out. You do still speak Vietnamese, don't you?"

The medic replied, "Yes, Sir." He took the old man by the shirt as the Captain had been holding him and dragged the old man off behind the hut. The Captain started working over another old man seeming to be really enjoying it, like one of the sadistic bastards I had to deal with back in school. I instantly hated this Captain.

Suddenly there was a shot and then an explosion behind the hut where Doc had taken the old man. All weapons came up to fire as Captain Carson yelled, "Hold your fire!" And we did.

Seconds after the explosion, there was another gunshot and we still held our fire even though our nerves were on edge.

The medic came from around the structure, blowing at the end of his forty-five. He created the illusion of what they did back in the Wild West after a shootout.

No words passed until he got to the Captain and then he announced, "I had no choice, sir. He pulled a grenade and I had to shoot him."

Captain Carson replied with a grin, "Well, we got the right village." I knew this was a ruse so the Captain would appear to be in the right.

The picture of what the medic had really done formed in my mind. It made me sick to think a medic could kill like that and enjoy it as this one seemed to be doing.

Captain Carson had the Vietnamese that hadn't gone into the hut forced in and then the Captain looked at me ordering, "Get the charges you need out of the APC and place them so this whole village goes up."

I asked, "With all the people inside?"

Sergeant Hicks spoke up, "No. A chopper will take them out before you blow it. Now get to work." So I did.

I slung my rifle and with Rebel's help, we placed a forty-pound shaped charge inside all the empty huts, and one just outside the occupied one to be placed inside later.

Then I ran my Det-cord around one and then another until I had them all on the same line.

I set the blasting cap to this and a fuse. I was ready when the choppers arrived. And then I reported to Hicks that I was ready.

Hicks just hung his head. He wouldn't even look at me nor acknowledge my reporting. Instead, Captain Carson told me, "Blow it, soldier!"

I spun around looking at the Captain and before I could respond, he repeated himself harshly. "Did you hear me, soldier! I said blow that village and now!"

I spoke as calmly as I could without moving, "With all the people still inside? There are women, children and old men in there who can't even fight back, as you've already found out." I knew instantly that I'd said too much with that last part.

The Captain glared at me with hate-filled eyes. I'd never seen that in a human being before. Then he further commanded, "Blow it or I'll put you in one and get someone else to blow it! It's your choice!"

I looked back at Hicks, who now looked at me and I told him, "I can't!"

Sergeant Hicks swallowed hard. Then told me, "Blow it, Ward. One of his men just told me that he's killed men for disobeying an order he gave."

I pleaded with Hicks, "But there's children and babies in there Sarge, I..."

Captain Carson's angry voice stopped me, causing my head to turn toward the Captain to find him pointing his forty-five pistol at my head demanding, "Do it!" And I could see in his eyes that he would shoot me. So I went to the fuse. I looked for Don, but he was nowhere in sight. Then using my lighter, I lit the fuse.

I walked past the Captain and Hicks to get my pack and find Don.

I found him sitting alone. So I sat down beside him as he dug into my pack. Half a minute later, when the village and its occupants blew up, I closed my eyes and Don stuck a needle into my arm and squeezed out its contents.

As the effect swept over me, Don remarked, "He's got the rank and you had no choice but to do what you were told. Right or wrong, it doesn't matter."

I opened my eyes, looking at him as the Morphine swept away all of the guilt I had felt. I knew I would never come down. I'd stay on my wonderful drugs and never have to think about what I'd just done ever again as I told Don, "At least they never knew what happened, even if they knew it was coming."

"See, you found something good out of it." And he was right, if there was to be any comfort in this. I nodded as we got up and crawled onto the APC and we were soon on our way.

Don and I not having a care in the world.

The APC stopped and when the engine turned off, I opened my eyes. It was dark! The rest of the day had passed and I didn't know it. But then too, I didn't care either.

I looked at my watch. But my eyes wouldn't adjust. I couldn't make out the time, but the effects of the Morphine were wearing off. Don would have to give me another shot soon.

Someone asked, "Hey. You guys going to eat before we move on in a few minutes?"

I reached over touching Don not knowing if he could see any

better, but we spoke almost in unison telling the guy, "Nah!" And then we started laughing.

Soon Jerry's voice inquired, "You two okay?"

Don declared, "Great, Jerry. But could you do us a favor and get us a couple C-rations? We're wasted and can't find a thing."

We started laughing at that and Jerry said, "Don't worry. I'll be right back."

Don and I laid there laughing, no longer even knowing why, nor caring. It just felt good doing so. We stopped when Jerry helped us sit up, giving each of us a can of hot rations. We ate them and found them to be surprisingly good for a change.

Word came that we would be moving out on foot, because the APC's and tank made too much noise for what was coming up next. Jerry helped us off the vehicle and into our gear, making us as ready as we were going to get for now.

We moved out and Jerry stayed close to us. Time no longer held any meaning and suddenly I felt like I could walk the rest of the night without a break. That is, until I saw Jerry drop to the ground. Don and I did the same, waiting to see why we had done so.

Nothing was said, so we cautiously followed Jerry to the rest of the group. We heard Captain Carson saying, "Point just reported activity ahead. So we're setting up an ambush here." We moved out, spreading a few meters apart. I tried to keep track of Captain Carson. I wanted to shoot him if and when a fire-fight started. But I got confused with all the movement of too many people moving about. So I figured I'd just wait for another chance to come. Because right now I was no longer sure of anything. But I now kept watch for enemy movement ahead.

Soon Sergeant Hicks came and told me, "Weaver. The Captain wants you out at the far end of the line. Take Jerry with you." Then he moved on.

Jerry came to me and we moved down the line to our new position. Jerry was following me and I realized the Captain wanted me dead. I wished it was Don with whom I was teamed. But Jerry and I had become friends, too. At least Hicks was sending someone with me that I knew. I was sure the Captain didn't know that piece of information.

As we approached Jerry's place to post, I heard a noise behind me. I turned and looked to see if Jerry was making it, wishing there was more moonlight to see by. For with what little light there was, I could barely see Jerry's silhouette behind me. At least, where he should have been, but he wasn't there.

I figured he must have tripped and fallen. So I backtracked to look for him.

I found someone I assumed to be Jerry laying on the ground. I knelt down and shook him, but got no reaction.

I found his wrists and checked for a pulse. But he was dead. But how?

As I started to check him further, lying my weapon aside and pulling my bayonet out to cut his gear away. It was the fastest way to allow me to find out what had killed him. Suddenly a voice loud and clear shouted, "Behind you, Ward! Look out!"

I had no way of knowing from where the voice had come. Nor did I recognize it. But I reacted upon it instantly. I turned and rose up at the same time and caught the blow glancing off my right shoulder.

It was something hard that had hit me. I went down, knowing that if I hadn't been turning and rising as I was, that blow would have taken me at the base of my skull, killing me! My shoulder hurt like hell and I knew that whoever had presented the blow, had killed Jerry.

Now the silhouette over me was raising an object to finish the job. I tightened my grip on my knife and kicked out hard with my left foot making contact with the object being swung down at me and the figure lost it.

The figure now dropped his knee against my chest, his hands finding my throat and started choking me.

As my left hand shoved against his chest, my right hand sent my bayonet into his midsections as hard as I could thrust it.

Then I quickly pulled it out thrusting it back inside and repeated this several times.

The hands around my throat loosened and I now shoved him sideways off me and laid there catching my breath and calming down.

I laid still, listening for any sounds of footsteps. Not hearing anything, I gathered myself and then found and picked up my weapon, positioning myself where I was.

The longer I waited, the more I thought about what had just happened and my body started shaking more violently than it ever had before.

Suddenly I doubled over in pain and fear, almost vomiting as my insides convulsed uncontrollably. I knew that if someone hadn't broken silence and warned me, I would have been lying next to Jerry dead. I determined in the morning, I would find the guy and thank him.

I heard a twig snap and I got ready to fire in that direction when a flicker of light showed someone ahead of me lighting a match and I knew it was none of us having made that kind of mistake.

As a fire was lit, a shot rang out and then everyone joined in. I found a target and shot.

I had only emptied a couple of clips when weapons in the camp dropped and hands flew into the air and the firing stopped, they had surrendered.

Figures moved in from the trees corralling the prisoners, stripping them of weapons and equipment before making them kneel lacing their fingers behind their heads.

They were secured and made to now sit in a group as the tank and APC's were brought up.

I reported to Hicks what had happened to Jerry and myself.

We found Jerry and the Vietnamese I'd killed where I had left them. Sergeant Hicks had Jerry's body placed inside the APC. Then I found Don telling him what had happened, including the guy that had warned me just in time and that I needed to find out who he was so I could thank him.

I asked around, but no one admitted to having said anything, nor even remember anyone calling out ahead of the shooting.

A few told me that if someone had broken silence and Captain Carson found out, he would literally string the guy up in a tree this morning. So I must have been hearing things, or imagined the whole thing, but my sore shoulder showed otherwise.

Even Sergeant Hicks told me, "You're lucky Jerry warned you before he died."

I informed him, "He couldn't have! I had already checked his pulse and he was dead before I was warned! So it had to be someone else. But no one will admit it so I can thank him."

Hick suggested, "Have you thought that maybe they could be just protecting themselves, knowing what that Captain would do if found out? Just be grateful." And I knew he was right. So I let it drop, wondering why these guys bothered to cover up for this Captain the way he treated them.

Don and I sat talking and he remarked, "I thought you came out here to look after me? But it looks like I'm going to have to start looking out for you."

I replied, "I welcome the help, but it looks like someone is beating you to it buddy. He just doesn't want to admit it."

Soon choppers showed up and Jerry's body along with others were placed aboard, along with the wounded. Other choppers taking on the prisoners and then we loaded up on the APC's and were on our way.

Don and I hadn't shot up this morning figuring with this Captain, we'd better keep our wits about us.

I felt relieved when the APC's found Highway One and turned South. This had to mean we were going home!

When we finally stopped in the loading area of our company, I was so happy, I almost got down and kissed the sand.

Going to the Hooch first, we cleaned our gear and put things away. Then we showered and went for supper.

Before Don and I went to bed, I told Don, "After this trip, I'm never going out again! No way!"

Don didn't answer, though I knew he heard me and we left it at that.

The next few days, Don and I stayed high, not wanting to deal with any of it.

Only having a few days left before going home, Don and I just ate and slept.

When the day came, I collected my souvenir rifle as we turned in our gear and then said good-bye to everyone. We caught a jeep to the Airstrip where we boarded a cargo plane to Cam Ranh Bay. Then we were aboard a Boeing 707 to start our long trip back across the ocean.

On the flight across, we saw the Sun go down, rise again, and almost fall before nearing the airport just outside Ft. Lewis, Washington. This time we had lost a day.

I was tired and just wanted to find a bathtub and soak in it for a week and then sleep for twice that long. But for some reason, I still had that nagging question playing hide-in-go-seek in the back of my mind as to why I was still alive? I guessed it was going to be the biggest "Why" I would ever have, until I found the answer.

As I rested, the voice I had heard warning me in the brush the night Jerry died, said, "Because I looked after you, Ward."

I jumped up out of my seat, looking around for whoever had said it, knowing it wasn't Don, for he was sleeping. But then too, so were most of the guys aboard: behind, in front, and beside us.

Seeing a guy two seats ahead of us reading a book, I called to him, "Hey! You reading that book!" He looked back at me and I inquired, "Excuse me, but did you just say something to me?"

He asked, "You talking to me?" I nodded and he shook his head answering, "Not me." Then he went back to reading his book and I figured someone was playing a joke on me, for the alternative wasn't acceptable.

As I relaxed, closing my eyes, the same voice announced, "I will always be with you." And I was either going crazy, or the Morphine was causing it. I wasn't sure.

At the airport, as we got off the plane, Don exclaimed, "Look at the 'Welcome Back Committee' waiting for us. Let's go meet our public buddy." Looking, I saw that there were a lot of people. But I was sure that they weren't there for us. They probably had family and friends on other flights coming in.

As we got to the end of the ramp coming off the plane, there was a roar of booing. Instantly we knew it was for us as they yelled obscenities at us.

We looked at each other, but kept walking toward the terminal.

Just as we all started to enter the building, a lady close by shouted, "How's it feel to be a baby killer you bastards?"

Rage surged through me as I looked at the lady that had spoken and started to respond, when Don quickly grabbed my arm telling me, "Don't pay them any attention. They're not worth it. Just keep going." I shrugged as a shower of rotten vegetables rained down on us from the crowd.

We rode the bus to the Base where a guy sitting behind a desk inside a big building took our papers instructing us, "Take a seat in the other room. Someone will be in shortly to talk to you. Then come back here and give me your name. I'll then give you a pass so you can go home."

We sat waiting and soon a Sergeant came in to address us. "I'm Sergeant Bails, as in Bails bonds. I know you're all anxious to go home. So here's what I am supposed to tell you:

Forget all the fighting and killing you've done for the past year. You're back in the States now and it won't be tolerated here. I'm supposed to make sure it's an order if need be. Now, in the other room there are coffee and cookies. Help yourself and welcome home. Your passes and further orders are waiting in the other room." And with that said, he left the room.

Don and I got our orders and passes, skipped the refreshments, and headed for the airport.

Our orders showed we would both be doing our last six months together at Ft. Riley, Kansas. So we said our goodbye's, shook hands and after getting our tickets home, we went our separate directions.

It wasn't long and I was wishing I'd changed into civilian clothes. Because as I passed a boy and I assumed his girlfriend, I heard the teenage girl say as she pointed at me, "Look Honey, one of those baby killers."

Suddenly, rather than being filled with rage, I wanted to run and hide. She was right. The image of that village flooded back into my mind.

I was angry and hated the Vietnamese people for not having killed me so I wouldn't have to go through life knowing that what these people were saying was the truth!

* * *

EPILOGUE

In the mountains of Northern California, there was a trailer house on a landing cut out of the side of the mountain by a bulldozer. It was an ordinary trailer in both color and design. A gravel road went up to the dwelling as a driveway and it hadn't changed since it had been put in.

Inside a couple occupied themselves as always at this time of the day: The man watching tv, while the woman cooked in the kitchen.

During an intermission, he asked the wife, "Have you heard from Ward today?"

She answered, "No. But I haven't been to the post office today either." She turned to take some food to the table and almost dropped the bowel. There before her, standing in the doorway was her son, Ward. Home from the Devil's Backyard.

www.ingramcontent.com/pod-product-compliance
Lightning Source LLC
Chambersburg PA
CBHW061607170626
46811CB00001B/354

* 9 7 8 1 9 4 9 5 7 6 3 2 0 *